PENGUIN BOOKS

You Don't Have What It Takes to Be My Nemesis

Praise for CAConrad's (Soma)tics

'Radical . . . This is poetry rooted in actual rituals involving nature, crystals, meditation and interactions with strangers. It is a response to the cruelties of the "rational" world . . . CAConrad's poems invite the reader to become an agent in a joint act of recovery, to step outside of passivity and propriety and to become susceptible to the illogical and the mysterious'

Tracy K. Smith, *The New York Times*

'CAConrad always argues (from the inside of their poems) for a poetry of radical inclusivity while keeping a very queer shoulder to the wheel. Their kind of queerness strikes me as nonpolarizing, not intentionally but because of the fullness of their exposition, a kind of gigantism that seems to me to be most deeply informed by love, and a tenderness for the ravages and tumult of existence'

Eileen Myles

'At a time when I don't always know how to make sense of what's going on, CAConrad serves as a cleareyed seer'

Jillian Steinhauer, *The New York Times*

Advance Praise

'In what is now the classic CAConrad mode of both exuberance and defiance, this book, like much of Conrad's epical body of work, is a tremendous ball of fire hurled into the dark recesses of our worlds (minds?). Luminous, sobering, but not without a capacious kindness in its ethos, this latest is a vibrant achievement from one of America's most legendary living poets'

Ocean Vuong, author of *Time Is a Mother*

'These are psychotropic, visionary songs of love and defiance. CA celebrates poetry as a connecting force, a spell-work which binds us to the earth, animals, stars, and one another'

Ralf Webb, author of *Rotten Days in Late Summer*

'Conjured in the extreme present, this is a vital addition to the global poetry canon. Through a lifetime of devotion to craft, Conrad has achieved an inventive and astonishing collection: a haunting, a prayer, a connection. They show how the ancient technology of poetry is between all things, living and not. Queer and gorgeous, filled with grief and belonging, a body within a body. Just stunning. I am dumb-struck'

Joelle Taylor, author of *C+nto: & Othered Poems*

'CAConrad's work is as tough and as vulnerable as our bodies, as intricate and blunt as a flattened copper penny or a lily of the valley or the nests we'd build if we were birds'

Luke Roberts, author of *Home Radio*

'I've been a fan of CAConrad's work from the beginning. There is always a necessary and vital life force at work in this poetry. This is a wondrous and essential selection of their noble life project'

Peter Gizzi, author of *Now It's Dark* and *Sky Burial: New and Selected Poems*

ABOUT THE AUTHOR

CAConrad has been working with the ancient technologies of poetry and ritual since 1975. They are the author of numerous poetry collections, including *The Book of Frank* (2010), *Ecodeviance: (Soma)tics for the Future Wilderness* (2014), *While Standing in Line for Death* (2017) and *Amanda Paradise: Resurrect Extinct Vibration* (2021), which won the PEN Josephine Miles Award. With Robert Dewhurst and Joshua Beckman, Conrad is the coeditor of *Supplication: Selected Poems of John Wieners* (2015). They have received a Creative Capital grant, a Pew Fellowship, a Lambda Literary Award, a Believer Magazine Book Award, a Gil Ott Book Award and, most recently, the 2022 Ruth Lilly Poetry Prize. Their life is the subject of the documentary *The Book of Conrad*, and their play *The Obituary Show* was made into a film in 2022 by Augusto Cascales.

After ten years on the road, Conrad currently lives in Greenfield, Massachusetts. They taught at UMass Amherst from Autumn 2022 to Spring 2023, and regularly teach at Columbia University in New York City and the Sandberg Art Institute in Amsterdam.

CACONRAD

You Don't Have What It Takes to Be My Nemesis

And Other (Soma)tics

PENGUIN BOOKS

PENGUIN BOOKS

UK | USA | Canada | Ireland | Australia
India | New Zealand | South Africa

Penguin Books is part of the Penguin Random House group of companies
whose addresses can be found at global.penguinrandomhouse.com.

First published in Penguin Books 2023
001

Set in 9.75/13.5pt Warnock Pro
Typeset by Jouve (UK), Milton Keynes
Printed and bound in Great Britain by Clays Ltd, Elcograf S.p.A.

The authorized representative in the EEA is Penguin Random House Ireland,
Morrison Chambers, 32 Nassau Street, Dublin D02 YH68

A CIP catalogue record for this book is available from the British Library

ISBN: 978–1–802–06245–8

www.greenpenguin.co.uk

for those open to
the transmission

This is a book of 24 (Soma)tic poetry rituals and their resulting poems. Contents by ritual:

CONTENTS

INTRODUCTION

I cannot stress enough how much this mechanistic world, as it becomes more and more efficient, resulting in ever-increasing brutality, has required me to find my body to find my planet in order to find my poetry. The last large wild beasts are being hunted, poisoned, asphyxiated in one way or another, and the transmission of their wildness is dying, taming. A desert is rising with this falling pulse.

I grew up in a working-class part of rural Pennsylvania. When my family works in the factories, they become extensions of the machines. They shut the present off to cope with their jobs, sending their minds into the past and future all day. When they go home, they cannot flip the switch back to the present, and when I speak with them, I hear that they are depressed about the past or anxious about the future, with no sense of the present. They extend the grind of their monotonous jobs outside the factory walls and into their lives, until they are no longer capable of accessing their artistic sensibilities.

This won't happen to me, I thought in my younger years, and moved to a large city to foster my skills as an artist and to surround myself with like-minded people. For many years this felt right: I was doing exactly what I came to do, not working in the factory back home. But in 2005 when visiting my family for a reunion I listened again to their stories about the factory. As always, they saddened me, and on the train ride home I had an epiphany. I realized that I had been treating my poetry like a factory, an assembly line, and doing so in many different ways, from how I constructed the poems, to my tabbed and sequenced folders for submissions to magazines. It was a crisis. I stopped writing for nearly a month, needing to figure out how to climb out of these factory-like structures, or to quit writing altogether. Understanding that in my childhood I had learned my family's coping mechanism of avoiding the present, I created (Soma)tic poetry rituals for a new relationship with time, as a way to more fully engage the everyday through writing.

Soma is an Indo-Persian word that means 'the divine'. *Somatic* is Greek. Its meaning translates as 'the tissue' or 'nervous system'. The goal is to bring together soma and somatic through the rituals, and to anchor me in the now, creating what I consider *an extreme present*. For the first ritual, I ate a single color of food each day for seven days and would also wear the color, starting with red. At the end of the first day with the red poem, I realized two important things: (1) I had remained present for the duration of the ritual. (2) I would have never written the red poem for any other reason. The orchestration of the ritual created the space for the language to appear. It was exhilarating, and I filled my days with rituals to write my poems.

It is our duty as poets and others who have not lost our jagged, creative edges to resist the urge to subdue our spirits and lose ourselves in the hypnotic beep of machines, of war, in the banal need for power and things. With our poems and creative core, we must return this world to its seismic levels of wildness.

CAConrad

I. A NEW (SOMA)TIC RITUAL

Listen to the Golden Boomerang Return

The first 9 poems were written from a (Soma)tic poetry ritual called *Listen to the Golden Boomerang Return*, working with creatures who have evolved to navigate the current state of the Anthropocene. Animals who not only survive under the imbalance of a human-centered world but have somehow found a way to thrive! I spent most of the COVID-19 lockdown in Seattle, a city overflowing with crows. Soon after I started feeding them on my window ledge, they began bringing me gifts of twigs, plastic, seeds, and gold stickers. While they shared the fresh fruit and nuts, I wrote while stroking my shoulders to embody their graceful wings. When I encounter coyotes, I scratch the back of my ears before writing, but with lizards, I rub my ankles and caress my jawline for squirrels. Embodying these creatures pushes my poetry onward.

Listen to the Golden Boomerang Return is what I have been working toward for many years, finding a way to fall in love with the world as it is, not as it was. We need new ways of appreciating the determination of life around us to realize better how this planet is worth whatever fight for it we offer. Each morning I watch the sunrise. Later in the day, I watch the sunrise on public outdoor webcams on other parts of our planet, like the Tokyo railyards, the astronomical clock of Prague, or the beautiful Byzantine mosque of Istanbul called Hagia Sophia. It takes nearly nine minutes for the light leaving the Sun to travel to Earth, bringing warmth, illumination, and essential nutrients for the health of our bones, blood, and immune systems. Ignition of cells in humans, other creatures, and plants is my focus for writing.

Part of this meditation on our planet's daily intake of our Sun's energy also involves spending time with wild plants growing through the cracks of sidewalks. Visiting abandoned shopping malls and centers across US-America offers many encounters with wild plants taking over the parking lots and wild creatures finding new homes. Deer, raccoons, sparrows, pigeons, rats, opossums, and cockroaches are some creatures I wrote with on my travels.

Listen to the Golden Boomerang Return is the most exciting (Soma)tic poetry ritual I have endeavored, and each day I am eager to push the language out of me with sunlight, wild animals, and plants to make new poems. Through my accumulation of outdoor webcams across the planet, I am eventually preparing to write poems through a continuous sunrise for 24 hours. The plan is to begin by waiting for the Sun to appear outside my door and then watch it unfold around the world online until it returns to my door again. The next day after my writing session through nonstop sunrise, I will work with a hypnotherapist to search my memory for the first time I saw the Sun as a child. I will then use the video documentation of being placed into the trance to continue my writing. The recall of my earliest contact with our star will expand the experience of watching our planet's sunrise for a full day.

to
desire
the world
as it is
not as
it was
falling
feather
attaches
to new life
for a moment
when the hammer
approached we thought
is that thing coming this way
we are the fractal
drop to hear
our own
harmonics
in the muffled
underground
hum of seeds

part of
this forest
tastes like
the man
I love
with an
actual number
of nails holding
the bedroom
together
other days
when we died
where we fell
we became
the forest
my car never
intended to be
a meat grinder
another face going
under the waves
we felt awful after
hitting the deer
we made love
and slept with
one of his
antlers
between
us

what was
the point
of today
nothing
more than
microscopic
creatures on
my eyelids
reaching for
sunlight with me
how hard is your
historical memory
as in gay
bashing 101
same day you
learn hieroglyph
means *sacred carving*
elegy is not a form
it is a state of being the
poet must write from
a faggot takes a beating
from another holy book
and the band said
this is my four leaf clover
what did they say
this is my four leaf clover

Do You Like
Your Species
is my latest
questionnaire
meet me at the
quarry where
Michelangelo
conjured David
adjusting
for machines
reaching for
emotions
switch inferno
for paradise
every cell
singing the
Ghost of
We Shall
Rise Again
if you call this planet
evil one more time
I will have to learn
to hold you better

our
little
places
within
are not
dungeons
remember
remember
astronomers point
satellites into space
the military points
them down at us
the inverse relationship
between love we offer
and what we give
this on and
off button
is another
opportunity
to believe
there are
only two
choices
this too
must end

mind and
body can only
be separated through
decapitation
another
mistake
we have
lived with
for too long
when it's your
turn go or
hesitate
which
will
it
be
I'm a poet
not a motivational speaker
I keep trying to tell you
press a hand to
the rumbling
wrap yourself in elegy
we kill 3000 silkworms
to make one
pound
of silk

refrigerators
are where
we keep our bodies
before they become
our bodies
spinning inside
routines this
living
provides
we sense
language
travel
on our
constant
breath
open a
friend's
refrigerator to yell
Hello Future Friend
human beings are a
symptom of the
Big Bang
gun
stores
fill with
shoppers
bombs mark
the sky with
our pledge

a potato
born by
shovel
I am a
bride of
poetry in
my orange
and purple
gown an
unequalled
extinction
machine
pushing
strollers through
ecosystems of
concrete and plastic
we camel through the journey
with our new playbook for
where plunging hands go
don't be weird
about this
you can be a
bride of
poetry
too

a shotgun above every
door where I grew up
I did not mean to
get her ashes
on my shoes
I will wait
to walk in
the rain
refusing
to exert the
stress of time
everyone envied
everyone's shotgun
behind their backs
our favorite game
when I was a baby
was to throw me
off the roof
then run
downstairs
to catch me
oh how we
laughed

II. . . . AND OTHER (SOMA)TICS

A Beautiful Marsupial Afternoon

2005–2010

Anoint Thyself

For John Coletti & Jess Mynes

Visit the home of a deceased poet you admire and bring some natural thing back with you. I went to Emily Dickinson's house the day after a reading event with my friend Susie Timmons. I scraped dirt from the foot of huge trees in the backyard into a little pot. We then drove into the woods where we found miniature pears, apples, and cherries to eat. I meditated in the arms of an oak tree with the pot of Emily's dirt, waking to the flutter of a red cardinal on a branch a foot or so from my face, staring, showing me his little tongue.

When I returned to Philadelphia I didn't shower for three days, then rubbed Emily's dirt all over my body, kneaded her rich Massachusetts soil deeply into my flesh, then put on my clothes and went out into the world. Every once in a while I stuck my nose inside the neck of my shirt to inhale her delicious, sweet earth covering me. I felt revirginized through the ceremony of my senses, I could feel her power tell me these are the ways to walk and speak and shift each glance into total concentration for maximum usage of our little allotment of time on a planet. LOSE AND WASTE NO MORE TIME POET! Lose and waste no more time she said to me as I took note after note on the world around me for the poem.

Emily Dickinson Came to
Earth and Then She Left

your sweaty party dress and my sweaty party
dress lasted a few minutes until the tomato
was gone someday they will disambiguate
you but not while I'm around our species
won Emily we won it feels so good to be win-
ning the flame of victory pass it around it
never goes out dinosaurs ruled Massachusetts dinosaurs fucking and laying eggs in
Amherst Boston Mount Holyoke then you
appeared high priestess pulling it out of the
goddamned garden with both hands you
Emily remembered the first time compre-
hending a struck match can spread a flame it
feels good to win this fair and square protest
my assessment all you want but not needing
to dream is like not needing to see the world
awaken to itself indestructible epiphanies
consume the path and just because you're
having fun doesn't mean you're not going to
die recrimination is the fruit to defy with unexpected appetite I will be your outsider if
that's how you need me electric company's
stupid threatening letters cannot affect a poet
who has faced death

Storm-Soaked Bread

For Julian Brolaski

Sit outside under shelter of a doorway, pavilion, or umbrella on a park bench, but somewhere outside where you can easily touch, smell, taste, FEEL the storm. Lean your face into the weather, face pointed UP to the sky, stay there for a bit with eyes closed while water fills the wells of your eyes. Come back into the shelter properly baptized in the beauty of pure elements and be quiet and still for a few minutes. Take some preliminary notes about your surroundings. Try not to engage with others who might run to your shelter for cover. If they insist on talking MOVE somewhere else; you are a poet with a storm to digest, this isn't time for small talk! You are not running from the storm, you are opening to it, you are IN IT! Stick a bare arm or foot into the storm, let your skin take in a meditative measure of wind and rain. If you are someone who RAN from storms in the past take time to examine the joys of the experience. Remind yourself you are a human being who is approximately 80 percent water SO WHAT'S THE HARM OF A FEW DROPS ON THE OUTSIDE!? Right? YES! Pause, hold your breath for a count of 4, then write with a FURY and without thinking, just let it FLOW OUT OF YOU, write, write, WRITE!

Set an empty cup in the storm, hold a slice of bread in the storm. Then put a little salt and pepper on your storm-soaked bread, maybe some oregano and garlic. With deliberate SLOOOWNESS chew your storm bread and drink the storm captured in your cup. Slowly. So, slowly, please, with, a, slowness, that, is, foreign, to, you. THINK the whole slow time of chewing and drinking how this water has been in a cycle for MILLIONS OF YEARS, falling to earth, quenching horses, elephants, lizards, dinosaurs, humans. They pissed, they died, their water evaporated and gathered again into clouds to drizzle down AND STORM DOWN into rivers, puddles, aqueducts, and ancient cupped hands.

Humans who LOVED, who are long dead, humans who thieved, raped, murdered, were generous, playful, disappointed, fearful, annoyed and adored one another, each of them dying in their own way, their water going back to the sky, coming back down to your bread, your lips, your stomach, to feed your sinew, your brain, your living, beautiful day. Take your notes POET, IT IS YOUR MOMENT to be totally aware, completely awake!

One Day I Will Step from the Beauty Parlor and Enlist in the Frequency of Starlings

my favorite morning
is not caring if
blood on sheets
is yours or mine

a machine in
your station
rides me
tracks to snacks
snacks to tracks

I feel very fortunate
to know magic is real
and poetry is real
you can see it in the writing if
a belief in one is missing

a mouse eating
the dead
cat our
longed-for
malfunction

I was born
in Topeka
otherwise
they would have
never let me in

they circle away holding this place
opening opening opening OPENING UP
I grope the tree down its root

if truth soothes
soothing was
not truth's goal

my goal
is to do what
produces
memory
as gentle
as vicious
can

one promise: when
I get to the bottom I'll
accelerate deeper
my small pile
of poems
surprising
everyone along the
open wound

'was there a
death' they ask
'a merger' I say

everyone paying attention
enjoy your visit
everyone else
good luck

Double-Shelter

For Joshua Beckman

thriving requires more than just survival.
  – Erica Kaufman

If you're preparing to visit someone far away, first spend time studying everyday structures of your own apartment. Where and HOW does the light hit walls? Press your ear to the refrigerator, taste the water with small sips, eyes open, eyes closed. Study the smell and temperature of rooms. Feel your pulse on the toilet, in the shower, by the oven. Cook broccoli with a little oil and salt. Eat it slowly.

As soon as you arrive at the house you are visiting cook broccoli with a little oil and salt. Eat it slowly. Do everything in reverse order, pressing your ear to the refrigerator. How is it different? Take notes while investigating THE TRUTH if there is truth. What does it mean to say THE TRUTH? What matters most? The water has what differences? Are they subtle? Metallic?

Listen to Philip Glass on the floor, on your back, very still, in, the, dark, just, you, and, Mr. Glass. I chose the song 'MUSIC IN CONTRARY MOTION'. Reflect on a personal violence you want undone. Some terrible THING that removed the beauty you once lived with. My boyfriend Mark (nicknamed Earth) moved to a queer community in Tennessee to work the land. He meditated in a cave each day where homophobic men followed him, bound and gagged him, covered him with gasoline, and set him on fire. For a long time I would go to sleep and dream of stabbing his murderers, shooting his murderers, drowning, choking, and bludgeoning his murderers. Breathtaking dreams of retribution for the man I loved, which, woke, me, each, morning, more inconsolable than the last. I was never going to feel happy again it seemed. Take notes about how the violence in your life will not leave. How it may never leave. Take notes about how you are sensing the world differently since then.

Express an Interest in Listening
or Flowers Won't Bother

greed it
seems
has no
memory

the little
bones they
throw us
break
my heart

some
days
i taste
the world
in a poem and
want
to be of
service
to that
taste

there is no doubt
the worst possible
things are possible

an epic
terrain of
anger no one
can move
out of you

it's best to let
flowers do
the talking

they say *write*
below your
century to
understand it

they say *crying*
in private helps
no one

they say *touch*
a gill of light
down there

they say *an*
asterisk is
the footnote
to a lie

they say *never*
use 'permanent'
in a sentence
containing
a noun

they say *if*
dancing is
prohibited
LEAVE
at once

from Mugged into Poetry

If you haven't been stabbed or shot, if they took your money under threat and left, consider a poem. After I was mugged recently in Philadelphia this exercise came to mind on the subway ride home, the postmugging subway ride when poetry took its rightful place at the center of my world where even muggers play a part in it, it being bigger than the knife, more concentrated and firmer than his cock which will have many admirers in prison. He's going to die. So am I. So are you. He could have EASILY killed me, he and his three friends BUT I AM ALIVE AND QUITE WELL writing for poetry as I willingly came to this cesspool of humanity to do. All the globe becomes a poem. It is enough to manage this small part, here, a body, in a body, stinking, beautiful, a bit of tormented, angry, tender, delicious flesh. It is enough. Each of us. If we can read this we are all alive and creative. Anyone who tells you that you are not creative is a coward afraid of his own potential, trust me. Ignore all cowards, they were born to be ignored. Find your strength, find your poems.

Every morning for 2 weeks as soon as you waken PREDICT your death. And write it down. For instance, 'by choking in 11 years, 4 months, 2 weeks, 6 days, 12:18 p.m.' THEN STARTING at the tips of your toes touch your cells of skin and nails, feel bones, your pulse, hair, feel your moving body in the morning ALWAYS moving as long as you live you are moving blood through veins moving thoughts through dreams EVERY morning for 2 weeks touch every inch of your body's surface and your holes moist and dry. As soon as you finish this reaffirming ritual write a poem from your moving blood in the thoughts of the dream, and combine that LIVING poem with the prediction of your death.

Guessing My Death

1

by choking in
11 years
4 months
2 weeks
6 days
12:18 p.m.

———

when i win the lottery
i want my legs amputated
and two beautiful peg legs
wooden of course

someone says it's
a very bad idea
he says i should
reconsider
seriously
reconsider

i want peg legs but
he says I'll regret it
he might be right

but what i really
want is to have my
real legs (the ones
i don't want)

cremated because
what i really want
is to scatter
my own
ashes

i thought about getting
liposuction and having
the fat cremated
but it's not
the same
because i can
eat more
delicious
doughnuts and
grow it back

it doesn't count

it HAS to be
something
missing for
good you
know

but to
spread my
own ashes is something
i love thinking about
and the cheerful
sound of my

peg legs on
Philadelphia
sidewalks

4

by stroke in
39 years
11 months
3 weeks
6 days
8:19 p.m.

———

FYI

your 45-minute
talk felt like
3 hours
i'm not a big
fan of similes
but it was
like listening to
Hedda Gabler
describe a
dental hygiene exam and after the first
hour and a half of
your 45 minutes
i prayed for
the angel of

death to break
through the
ceiling and
snatch me
away

6

by nuclear missile in
2 years
2 months
3 weeks
6 days
9:47 a.m.

———

i convinced my
sometimes-boyfriend
Peanut to swallow
a beautiful quartz
gemstone

it came to me to
have it pass through
Peanut's body
then

clean it
swallow it myself

this special stone's
specialness increased
from passing
through
our bodies

it will vibrate of
our shared
pregnancy

two men in
love three
times a week
sometimes
four times

7

by falling into an elevator shaft in
6 years
4 months
2 weeks
5 days
midnight

———

dream of frying giant leaves with christina strong at her new home in hawaii pink
little pink (NEON PINK) butterflies fly out of the leaves as we cook them she says
it's a good sign i ask her if she's sure she says while waving a freshly lit joint NEVER
DOUBT A BUTTERFLY CONRAD!

second part of dream i fly into NY from hawaii and christina meets me at airport we take subway into town there are advertisements for lockheed martin on train i say CHRISTINA THERE ARE ADS FOR LOCKHEED MARTIN she says I KNOW I KNOW i asked WHY THOUGH WHY ON EARTH she says WHILE YOU WERE AWAY WAR ENDED AND NOW THEY NEED TO ADVERTISE BECAUSE OF WORLD PEACE it was the most exciting news ever we got off at 2nd Ave and there were thousands of people hugging in the streets

(some dreams like this dream i want to reenact exactly)

8

by electrocution in
4 years
11 months
1 week
1 day
4:13 a.m.

———

i really
love moving
while
standing still
sitting still
i do it by
escalator
bus
airplane
elevator
horse

car
train
trolley
LSD

(must admit most of
my acid trips have
been evil i need
a lighter trip
diet LSD)

9

by wild dogs in
14 years
7 months
3 weeks
2 days
1:00 a.m.

———

there were four of them it was the strangest mugging i was going to a poetry reading in philadelphia walked the wrong way they called out from behind me as if they knew me the one with the knife came around first 'AW, HEY, HE'S A DUDE!' a little confused by my long hair bright green shirt purple glitter nail polish two were behind me while another faced me and asked

   'are you gay?'
   'yes'
   'my cousin is gay'
   'do you like your cousin?'

'yeah, my cousin's cool, i LOVE my family'

while the one with the knife pointed at my heart then my stomach jerking in his hand pointed at my head then my groin he was irritated by our conversation 'JUST GIVE ME YOUR WALLET MAN!' he found only twelve dollars 'TWELVE DOLLARS IS ALL YOU GOT!?' the one who likes his gay cousin said 'just take the cash, cards are hard to replace' they argued but took only the cash dropped the wallet ran off three dollars for each of them but it was a gay-positive mugging

XX

a little note at the end of this series of poems:

i'm going to have
a samosa-eating
contest with
myself but before
i do oh people
of the future
i am so angry
that you walk
beautiful with life
my city's streets
without me after
i die but go to
my favorite
corner please
and wave at
the sky please
22nd & Chestnut Streets, Philadelphia, Pennsylvania,
United States of America, Planet Earth, Milky Way Galaxy, the Universe

Touch Yourself for Art

For Penny Arcade

There must be a piece of art near where you live that you enjoy, even LOVE! A piece of art that IF THERE WAS WAR you would steal it and hide it in your little apartment. I'm going to PACK my apartment TO THE ROOF when war comes! This exercise needs 7 days, but not 7 consecutive days as most museums and galleries are not open 7 days a week. At the Philadelphia Museum of Art hangs the Mark Rothko 'Orange, Red and Yellow, 1961' a painting I would marry and cherish in sickness and in health, have its little Rothko babies, and hang them on the wall with their father. But I'm not allowed to even touch it! The security guards will think you're as weird as they think I am when you come for 7 days to sit and meditate. Never mind that, bribe them with candy, cigarettes or soda, whatever it takes to be left in peace. For 7 days I sat with my dearest Rothko.

Bring binoculars because you will get closer to the painting than anyone else in the room! Feel free to fall in love with what you see, you're a poet, you're writing a poem, go ahead and fall in love! Feel free to go to the museum restroom and touch yourself in the stall, and be sure to write on the wall that you were there and what you were doing as everyone enjoys a dedication to details in the museum. And be certain to leave your number, you never know what other art lover will be reading. Return with your binoculars. There is no museum in the world with rules against the use of binoculars, information you may need for the guards if you run out of cigarettes and candy.

Map your 7 days with physical treats to enhance your experience: mint leaves to suck, chocolate liqueurs, cotton balls between your toes, firm-fitting satin underwear, things you can rock-out with in secret for the art you love. Take notes, there must be a concentration on notes in your pleasure making. Never mind how horrifying your notes may become, horror and pleasure have an illogical mix when you touch yourself for art. When you gather your 7 days of notes you will see the poem waiting in there. Pull it out like pulling yourself out of a long and energizing dream.

Rothko7

Whether things wither or whether your ability to see them does.
– from 'The Coinciding', by Carrie Hunter

DAY 1

it's
October
I pressed
this buttercup in April
I DON'T CARE WHAT YOU THINK
call me it!
call me sentimental!
HAVE YOU SEEN THE HEADLINES?
spring is a
luxury
I hope
for another to
garden with my
bare hands

DAY 2

awkwardness of being insane
arrives
after
diagnosis
not before
remove description
from the splendor
do not hesitate

DAY 3

more of a ghost
than my ghosts
here I am

DAY 4

tablet on tongue
stray voltage catching
my ankles

ready to marry
the chopped
off head

while elaborate in curse
it contributes evidence
of life

DAY 5

he kissed me while
I sang
refrain shoved
against epiglottis

centuries of a vowel for
endless refutable corrections
puts mouth
to want

DAY 6

songs dying bodies sing at
involuntary
junctures of
living

EXIT sign
leads us to empty
launch pad
walking
maybe
walking
maybe or riding
the collapsing tower

big hands of
big clock missing
this is not symbolism
they were gone

DAY 7

I'm not tearing back
curtains looking
I know Love is
on the other
side of
town

burying the leash
with the dog was
nothing but
cruel don't ever
speak to me again
help me stop
dreaming your
destruction

Confetti Allegiance

Is there a deceased poet who was alive in your lifetime but you never met, and you wish you had met? A poet you would LOVE to correspond with, but it's too late? Take notes about this missed opportunity. What is your favorite poem by this poet? Write it on unlined paper by hand (no typing). If we were gods we wouldn't need to invent beautiful poems, and that's why our lives are more interesting, and that's why the gods are always meddling in our affairs out of boredom. It's like the fascination the rich have with the poor. As Alice Notley says, 'The poor are more interesting than others, almost uniformly.' This poem was written by a human poet, and we humans love our poets, if we have any sense. Does something strike flint in you from the process of engaging your body to write this poem you know and love? Notes, notes, take notes.

The poet for me in doing this exercise is Jim Brodey and his poem 'Little Light', which he wrote in the bathtub while listening to the music of Eric Dolphy, masturbating in the middle of the poem, 'while the soot-tinted noise of too-full streets echoes / and I pick up the quietly diminishing soap & do / myself again'. Take your handwritten version of the poem and cut it into tiny confetti. Heat olive oil in a frying pan and toss the confetti poem in. Add garlic, onion, parsnip, whatever you want, pepper it, salt it, serve it over noodles or rice. Eat the delicious poem with a nice glass of red wine, pausing to read it out loud and toast the poet, 'MANY APOLOGIES FOR NOT TOASTING YOU WHEN YOU WERE ALIVE!' Take notes while slowly chewing the poem. Chew slowly so your saliva breaks the poem down before it slides into your belly to feed your blood and cells of your body. Gather your notes, write your poem.

Love Letter to Jim Brodey

Dear Jim
for
those whose
acid trips were a success
only twice
I've met men who
are high exactly
as they are sober
both became my lovers

both died one like
you died Jim he
played music too
loud at parties to
gather us into a
single frequency feel
healed for the length
of a song

nothing works forever
there was something in
the air that year Jim
and you put it there

a rapt center in
pivot looking
to face
Love again

learning to
accept what's offered
without guilt

to be reminded
of nothing
my favorite day not dragging
the dead around

they're looking
for Lorca in the Valley
of the Fallen

Franco's thugs would understand
'developing countries' means
getting them ready for
mining diamonds drilling oil
teaching them to make a
decent cup of coffee for
visiting executives

if I'm not going
to live like this
anymore I must will
every cell to
stand away

the *History of Madness*
725 pages is too much to
not be normal

scorn is very
motivating

       I'm vegetarian unless
       angels are on the
       menu mouthwatering
       deep-fried wings
       shove greasy bones in
       their trumpets

the cost of
       scorn is
       often unexpected

       I see my fascist
neighbor from downstairs
'Did my boyfriend and
I make too much
noise last night?'
his glare the
YES that keeps
me smiling

Ecodeviance:
(Soma)tics for the Future Wilderness

2010–2013

M. I. A. Escalator

For Jen Benka & Carol Mirakove

I rode several of my favorite escalators in Philadelphia, taking notes up and down the vantages. At the top and bottom of the ride I would show photographs of myself to strangers and ask, 'EXCUSE ME, have you seen this person?' Sometimes there was confusion, 'ISN'T THAT YOU?' I would reply, 'No, many people think I look like HER, but have you seen HER?' I feel very fortunate to have been born BEFORE the ultrasound machine. My generation was the last generation to have a male and female name waiting at the other end of the birth canal. My generation is the last to have our mothers touch their bellies talking to us as male and female. Pink or blue?

Both pink and blue, 'Have you seen this person?' I enjoyed my conversations with strangers and made at least one new friend, a handsome man who knew I was the person in the photograph. That person, I am that person and agreed. The ultrasound machine gives the parents the ability to talk to the unborn by their gender, taking the intersexed nine-month conversation away from the child. The opportunities limit us in our new world. Encourage parents to not know, encourage parents to allow anticipation on either end. Escalators are a nice ride, slowly rising and falling, writing while riding, notes for the poem, meeting new people at either end, 'Excuse me, EXCUSE ME . . .' My escalator notes became a poem.

I Hope I'm Loud When I'm Dead

I have a
mannequin for
a paperweight
it is difficult to
type with such a
large paperweight
I reach around
lovers late into
night typing
from behind it is
impossible to
tell which
is Virgil
poetry
can be
of use
the field of flying
bullets the hand
reaches through
loving the aftertaste
finding a deeper
third taste
many are
haunted by
human cruelty through
the centuries
I am haunted by
our actions since
breakfast
you said *too much poetry*
I said *too much war*
the biggest mistake for

love is straining
there was a
door marked
MISTAKE we
entered
you said *too much fooling around*
I said *fuck off and die*

Security Cameras and Flowers Dreaming the Elevation Allegiance

For Susie Timmons

From Walnut & Broad St. to Walnut & 19th I stopped for every security camera. Philadelphia watches us always, FUCK YOU WATCHING US ALWAYS!! Several cameras in one block. I took notes, it was noon it was twelve just as I wanted it to be. I took notes for the poem, notes notes notes.

A little basket of edible flowers: nasturtiums, roses, pansies. I eat pansies, I LOVE pansies, they're delicious buttery purple lettuce!! At each security camera I paused, looked into the camera, DIRECTLY IN THERE, and stuck my tongue inside a flower. Flicked it in and out, in and out, flicking, licking, suckling blossoms. A security guard asked, *'What the fuck are YOU DOING?'* I replied, 'I'M A POLLI-NATOR, I'M A POLLINATOR!!' I allowed myself to say only this for the duration of the security camera pollination application, 'I'M A POLLINATOR, I'M A POL-LINATOR!!' I took many notes, and the notes became a poem titled, 'I WANT TO DO EVERY / THING WRONG JUST ONCE.'

I Want to Do Every
Thing Wrong Just Once

suddenly we are
a daisy under
the big wheel
throw it out to the batter leave it up to the outfield
the umpire sees how I divide you from me
you have no choice over the
weak notes in the song
you think I'm afraid
of course I am
I'm disgusted chopping us in two
                    will it help to
                    kill the one who
                    hypnotizes you?
                    We can try
                    we can always try
betting on the better point of quaking
we cap the balding yard with angel wings ancient astronauts
a poetic acuity we have been waiting to carry us away forever
        to survive I stayed away from
            people who wanted to
                kill me (that's
                the big secret)
                let them jam it
                in the back of your
                mouth just a quick
                police search

from Preternatural Conversations

For Dana Ward

Every once in a while I think something about a stranger on the sidewalk and they dart a glance at me and I get it – I GET IT – we are one! Allow seven consecutive days for this exercise. DAY ONE, think about a woman you know, think about experiences you have had with her. Think about conversations you have had, think about the things she wears, eats, her way of walking, her laugh. Think about every detail you can imagine. See if she calls you or e-mails you. Take notes about this attempt at psychic connection.

DAY TWO, do everything you did in DAY ONE, but for a man you know. DAY THREE, go out to the streets and follow someone walking a dog. Look closely at the dog, study the dog's movements. Whistle in your head, bark in your head. Imagine throwing a stick, yelling 'GOOD DOG! GOOD DOG! YOU ARE A VERY GOOD DOG!' Does the dog respond to this? If so, how? Take notes.

DAYS FOUR, FIVE, SIX, and SEVEN are for strangers. In cafés or restaurants, or followed briefly on the sidewalk. Try to connect with two women and two men, complete strangers out in the world. Study them in cafés, museums, going up escalators, or maybe standing in line at the bank. Aim your attention at the clothing they wear or the way they chew food. Envision saying HELLO, tugging their sleeve. TUG IT with your mind, punctuated with putting an imaginary hand on their shoulder and saying, 'Don't I know you?' Imagine clapping and shouting 'HEY! HEY! HEY YOU!' Did they look at you WHILE you were walking behind them? Communicating beyond the auditory is our goal. What are their reactions? How do you feel about it? Take these seven days of notes and form your poem(s).

I don't offer
frayed blooms while
caring for the center
I love my liver
my gallbladder
pat them good
morning through flesh
I want to show my
kidneys this sunrise
they deserve it working
hard take them out OUCH
see the pretty red
and pink OUCH sky
love you love you
sew you back
my spirit starts
chiming into the wind my
craving for wonder

Ed Dorn says
faggots should drink directly
from the sewer
I want to dress
special for this
finger wilderness
in his beard
I.V. drip of
sphinx's blood
'what camouflage
will you wear to hide
in the gingerbread
house?' he asks
'none, I want the witch
to find me EAT ME!'
I prefer a song where
I am fed, 'Oh Ed,
if you can't handle
me calling you my
sister I don't need
a brother'

if I had been
there when they
invented the word
chair
things would
be different would sound better
look at this amazing
structure holding
our bodies in place
to write
to quarrel with ourselves and others
to eat and sing
to launch forth new ideas
to comfort the sphincter
chair is a ridiculous word
monosyllabic NONSENSE
I love chairs but remain
annoyed by their name
living in this post-vocabulary
chosen without
imagination
chair chair chair CHAIR
nothing less than
seven syllables will do

Equinox Eve

SILENT MEETING GROUP

For Allison Cobb & Jennifer Coleman

Over seven billion human beings live on Earth now. We have displaced or made extinct so many other species of animals, insects, and plants that we have actually lost track! In the age of Emily Dickinson less than a billion humans were alive and wild bison roamed the open plains of the United States. Today there is just a small herd grazing in Yellowstone National Park, and those were put there to be wild on purpose. Same with the wolves, also exterminated from the land, and now reintroduced by way of the park system. These animals are not wild they are museums of fur, hooves, and fangs, part of a well-managed safari rather than wilderness. We love our museums, they comfort and soothe us when we feel uncertain of the choices we have made.

This (Soma)tic ritual gets us a little closer to how strange and troubled we humans are. I made a flier and hung it all over Philadelphia:

SILENT MEETING GROUP
WEDNESDAY, MARCH 20th
5PM TO 6PM
2nd FLOOR COUCH AREA OF
THE BOOK TRADER
(2nd ST. & MARKET ST.)
ONLY RULE: NO TALKING

There are only a few places where strangers can respectably be together in silence: on an elevator, at the movies, waiting for a bus, waiting to pay at the store. But to come together for the purpose of being quiet, to study one another for a full hour, that is something very different. As much as 80 percent of human communication is nonverbal, remember this detail. Do not fear looking at the people who show up because we all came to look and be looked at.

Twelve people participated, some of them quite odd looking, and one young Goth teen who glared at us with a sneer. Several were uncomfortable at the ten-minute mark, and they closed their eyes to meditate, or to appear to be meditating, but their eyes were closed for the rest of the hour. As soon as the hour was up I casually walked away WITHOUT TALKING! It's important to GO, GET GOING, GO SOMEWHERE where you can sit and quietly take account of your silent meeting. Take the quiet with you to write your poem.

Ecodeviance

dear glen of
goldenrod
I would have
your abortion
not being devoted to the way
things appear
you want me to
be fearless but
I cannot relax in
your world I can
go home where
success collides with
all the bad
behavior that
fed me to the
tyranny of the
chrysalis
you ask if
Shakespeare
was queer
I say the love of
his Juliet and his
Romeo was as
outlaw as it gets
devoted to the way
things are means the
odds are bad
sometimes white men
with long hair nod to
me downtown because
I'm a white man with
long hair

you think
having your
abortion means
I love you
what can
I say

from Full Moon Hawk Application

everlastingly stronger
on top of the moon
  – Alfred Starr Hamilton

I had the privilege of spending a month in the Leighton Artist Colony's Hemingway Studio at Banff Centre, located in the Canadian Rockies. In ancient times First Nations people used Banff as a locus for healing their sick, but they refused to live there. Banff Centre sits atop an enormous deposit of magnetic iron. Many holistic health practitioners use magnets to pull toxins out of the tissue and into the blood to then be flushed from the body. Here we are catching up with ancestral wisdom, finally.

This (Soma)tic poetry ritual resulted in a series of apologue poems without a definitive statement, the moral caught in a fang in a tree. Every morning I would meditate on a Philadelphia webcam poised on redtail hawks and their three chicks nesting on a window ledge of the Benjamin Franklin Institute. It was ridiculous leaving Philadelphia to visit it via webcam every single morning in western Canada, but the ridiculous world's exertions is what I sought to unzip the sublime. I wrote inside the hawk application, writing through the Philadelphia webcam. One day my boyfriend Rich appeared on the camera, waving from the street below the nest, then opened his sign FUCK YOU COME HOME!

A young man named Freddie drove me to the top of the mountains above the art colony to show me the hot springs and lake. There were fish in the lake, fish swimming above our heads at Banff Centre, and this became part of my (Soma)tic ritual. I would go to sleep with a piece of celestite crystal, meditating on the swimming above me, *the swimming above me! OREAD FREQUENCIES!* The notes for the poems were often informed by nightmares, the magnetic iron dumping toxins into my blood, making sleep difficult. A few nights it seemed I didn't sleep at all, but was instead dreaming about not sleeping. Once I dreamed I had a cunt for a nose, and that was fantastic, putting fingers in the cunt of my face!

After notes from the morning hawk webcam meditations I brushed my gums vigorously with cayenne pepper to stimulate the capillaries, JOLT the heart. I then drank a glass of crystal-infused water, the glass flanked by a four-inch shaft of citrine, a two-inch pyramid of selenite, and dangling just above the surface was a piece of the ancient Russian meteorite known as seraphinite. The citrine and selenite pulled negative charge from the water while seraphinite infused it with the angelic order to trigger my spinal cord into epiphanic alignment.

Mountain lion paw prints in fresh snow, grizzly bear scat, elk, mink, a pack of beautiful coyotes, and the magnificent magpies were outside my studio in the forest. It would be easy to write nature poems, documentary poems, straight-up narrative poems, but my notes were for poems found in the greasy film along the engines of our planetary machine coughing, devouring, running in terror. My unease of hungry mountain lions, grizzlies, and angry elk fueled the notes. A strict vegan diet with deep-tissue shiatsu massage once a week also contributed to the lens I brought to the notes for the poems. Banff was scraping me clean each day, and I kept to the flow, kept the image of fish swimming above my head, the hawks feeding their young, and the crystals I slept with on the full moon for the final hawk application. The notes became 13 poems for 13 moons. The editing process for the poems included listening to three original movie soundtracks played simultaneously: *Paris Texas*, *The Assassination of Jesse James*, and *Brokeback Mountain*.

Reading Starlight with One Eye Like Creeley

hearing all bells at
once instructs the final exhale
Camelot in thimble of the gods
Marilyn Monroe's ambulance
lost on the way to the palace of temperament
a branch of government for the magical arts
punch wall of forest for
an oaken
desk
another dream we
needed agitating the
sentence as it rows across a
newly destroyed heart folding
following tormenting one another
we were all once young and
beautiful squandering everything
it's what we came here to do
cut off engines to the child
registering disposition of
cat in the dark as the
size of the darkness

Did You Ever Forget Someone Can't Help You
Because They're Dead I'm Boring Like That

we can never oversimplify the
way it will occur making me
friend like a friend in the dark
my plot to cover the place with tenderness
a planet coping with seven billion
human breaths a second no
exit route planned not sure
if what we do to live will
smash us to dust
hawks washing through our veins
tongues pressed to spiderwebs
I love the way we are
high together trying to
shout ourselves off the
map *this is dangerous* you say
I hit the fallen snow with a
banana over and over chanting
THIS TROPICAL FRUIT NOW KNOWS THE ICE CRYSTAL
THIS TROPICAL FRUIT NOW KNOWS THE ICE CRYSTAL
THIS TROPICAL FRUIT NOW KNOWS THE ICE CRYSTAL
THIS TROPICAL FRUIT NOW KNOWS THE ICE CRYSTAL

All the Books Holding
Back Our Enemies

my integument
breach is substantial
not to brag
killing off the coastline
I can't stop myself from
butchering it all
your smell is nice
keep me under your coat awhile
you are warmer than I have ever been
smell better than I have ever smelled
ask anybody outside this
intermediate station of
the waist-high demon
garlands of dead
children for the pentagon
catharsis is a daughter
a son a caterwaul
soon we fall apart we
were hoping to do so
vomit in folders with
the purple tabs
vocabulary after
death has a different
present tense
vowels out of range

Enough Cocaine for
a Snow Angel

I worry about gravy my body will
produce in the crematorium
is this embarrassment morbid
burn me with the box or
dump me into a frying pan
this thinking makes a hole in the noun
am I supposed to
apologize I never
know when it's
time for sorry
I'm tired of fucking around we need
action is that the right thing to need
ebullience of being a lion tonight
I'm coming at you my dear
get the whip get the chair
look scared look scared
no meat no meat
throw me broccoli
throw me kale
green pussy
green green green pussy
I'm gonna be
green pussy

Who Punishes Us More than the Sad Eyes of Our Victims

when humans
trust weeds
know them
hear
tone of grass see visions of
milking their blades to
blend with ordinary
gentleness of wind
ketamine has
nothing on my
dreaming it's a good
time some other
bastard can have
this planet
is what they
told us it would be
a French pair of French fervency
scent of delicious French armpits
Alice paused to face Gertrude
you know how to grab me throw me under
your indelicate disposition you are like
swallowing a needle in search of thread
but you won't put that in your
book of what you say I say

Lonely Deep Affection

years of practice for a soft
landing in the slaughter
we looked far off to
a flag sewn into flesh
dear enemy come down the
hill I have taken a title out
of the love for you jumping
down the clear shaft of your eye
you would not know how long I
paused when writing this unless
I said so in the poem
half an hour staring
at the pencil having
written of my enemy with
love and fight to maintain
the ascension
voices from a
room no one exits
we pry genocide out
of the museum but
meant to remove
the museum
from genocide

Painted Pigeon Project

For Candice Lin

Find a photograph of a bird living far from where you live. I received a photo of a beautiful, truly extraordinary pigeon who lives near the Rialto Bridge in Venice. She has turquoise, chartreuse, and other shades of green and blue, painted with food coloring by artists. Print the photo and flutter it above your head, hold it to trees, rocks, ledges, imagining, imagining, imagining!! I painted my hand colors of the Venetian beauty, cooing when hand snuggled inside a pocket. I took notes while eating seeds offered from my pigeon hand. Pigeon hand is not a condition any more than art is a condition.

Save hair from your brush and roll it into a nice soft ball, then wash it. Insert a few seeds of flax, pumpkin, and caraway, something delicious. Pour more seeds on the ground, hair tucked in the center. Wait and watch. Soon enough a bird will carry it off to cushion their nest. Try to be patient and watch for them, try to see them. Write down EXACTLY what they looked like, where they flew off to, and keep that writing on you at all times. Take it out of your pocket and read it. Read it before going off to sleep at night. DREAM of the nest by thinking about these small, feathered creatures sleeping on your hair, and touch your hair while falling off to sleep, you and the birds, sleeping and dreaming together. WAKE and write as fast as you can, WAKE and write, wake and WRITE!! The notes become the poem.

Now Only 30% Taphephobic
Feeling Better by Open Holes

                              future war
                              pains me to
                              touch off this
                              diving board
                         drawn to make it living
you said we must not think of a gloomy world
we must not live in the present I think you mean
                    will angle with bees in the field
                    will explore child's mind in math lab
                    someone shatters their heart at
                    the microphone and we
                    go with them a bunch of
                    maudlin spectators we can't
                    leave it inside the sentence
                    pull it off the paper make a
                    door in woodshop shut it out
          babies born in war melt out of this hell
          stop them from entering the sentence
                         the only man I wanted to
                         grow old with was killed in
                         the hills of Tennessee
                         dreaming head to head
                         across night together
                         whistles branding
                         air around us
               ordered in the execrable
               another near miss of mortar shell
               I blame everyone when I blame
               myself I'm that good a shot
               fuck you we got you now
               gangster coffin with a

presidential seal may you keep
fleeing the underworld in vain
farmers of the patch of clean white
paper what made you spell my
name before I was ready
too bad too bad too bad
mom did jesus have pubes
jesus didn't have a cock honey

from Translucent Salamander

For Eileen Myles

the cynic and the killer waltz together
  – from a song my grandmother sang

Wyoming is the least inhabited of the fifty states. I was excited to see the night sky
at Ucross Foundation. Each night I sat waiting for the stars. I noted the first and
brightest above distant hills, above branches, and as others twinkled into view I
created my own constellations. Eighteen in all, and each constellation demanded
a different toll to pay at the start of my note taking. For instance the fifth toll of Xal-
lan was paid by meditating with a fist of citrine stone in my left hand. The toll of
stars over Ucross was always paid in meditating with stones. Celestite, purchased
in Boulder, Colorado, is a gem used to communicate with spirit guides some call
angels. Clear quartz, a gift from poet Elizabeth Willis, was a translucent mirror
where the salamander appeared in a waking dream. The citrine I purchased at the
Edgar Cayce Institute cleaned negative charge and led the way to understanding
the wealth of this organic body named Ucross where deer, mink, golden eagles,
sheep, rabbits, mice, and thousands of insects, plants, stones, worms, birds, and
other living beings thrive in their own unimpeded cycles. One night a great horned
owl dropped a mouse at my feet. I wrote, 'it doesn't have to mean something / but
it probably does.' I would write my notes while staring into a constellation with
a gemstone in my left hand. Not since my childhood in rural Pennsylvania have
I spent this much time staring into the Milky Way. And as I did as a boy, I would
STARE AT ONE STAR for as long as it took to SUDDENLY SEE, for just a second, ALL OF THEM AT ONCE!!

Hammering the notes into one document the next morning started with drinking a drop of Lemurian quartz. Barry David of Mount Shasta makes gemstone infusions under the full moon with mountain spring water and crystal essence. This is the same crystal I wear around my neck, a Lemurian quartz. I also wore a rotating scent of sandalwood, cedar, and rose. Sandalwood has a high frequency that aligns the chakras and enhances cellular vibration for spiritual awareness. Cedar helps eliminate mental and spiritual obstructions and stagnation for clearer and more harmonious creative channels. Rose has the highest hertz measurements of any living being on Earth, and its scent will immediately clear the heart chakra, making it a portal for psychic transmission and reception. Each day I rotated these oils, a dab on the third eye, the wrists, the soles of my feet, and with a sip of Lemurian quartz I would BEGIN!!

At noon when lunch arrived I would take the fruit from the bag, set it on the floor with my laptop, then play one of the eight songs on the album Cathedral City by the musical genius of VICTOIRE, composed by Missy Mazzoli. The music of Cathedral City was perfect as a vehicle to channel my constellation notes into poems. I would cover the piece of fruit and laptop with a basket, then with a blanket, then with pillows, then with towels, and finally with a large comforter, then PLAY THE MUSIC AS LOUD AS I COULD. It was inaudible from all the coverings that were keeping the music CLOSE to the piece of fruit and INFUSING its water molecules with VICTOIRE!! As soon as the song was finished I ATE THE FRUIT as quickly as possible while the song was still deep inside its flesh. Eating song in fruit, EATING SONG!! I then set about with the first phase of dividing my notes into language for poetry. In the sunlight I would lie on my back, my head over the edge of the deck, to SEE the beautiful pastures and quaking aspen upside down. The upside-down view was for the second phase of dividing my notes into language for poetry. I would look back and forth between the upside-down beautiful world, and the notes, until the notes were picked clean of excrescence and the shining teeth came clear in the skull.

In late afternoon I would wash my crystals in peppermint soap and set them in the sun to dry and collect nutrient-rich light. A sheep I named Gabriella, after one of my constellations, would always approach her fence closest to the gemstones. One day a flock of agitated migrating starlings surrounded them, singing WILDLY into them!! For weeks the eighteen poems were created and later sculpted, one for each of my eighteen constellations over Wyoming skies. Part of my meditation wandered from the beauty of this natural setting to remember how it is people have destroyed so much land that Ucross seems an oasis. We have been mistaken for centuries about our lives on Earth. Early white men named Yosemite National Park, thinking it was the name of the native Miwok people who first lived there. Yosemite actually means 'Killers, those to be feared'. One of our great national parks is named after a description of who we have turned out to be, clawing our way through untold reserves of natural resources, killing all life that gets in the way.

Wondering About Our Demise While Driving to Disneyland with Abandon

don't be
afraid of
all we have pending
plasma I sold
in Albuquerque
broke even with
food I purchased to produce it
we can manage we can start under
this tree a quiet hour of
dozing into the bark will
reveal the step forward
things thinking about each other
this crystal and feather
ask me to bring them
together put them behind
the books they want a
private conversation and
that means me getting lost to
fellowship with grass soil and little
stones who tell me there is no clear
sense of when we leave this world
an owl drops a mouse in front of me
it doesn't have to mean something
but it probably does
help fishing a glass eye out of
the garbage disposal was my
favorite time helping anyone
he was so happy pushing it
back into his head shaking
my hand at the same time
we both wished he wasn't
my boyfriend's brother

Our Planet to the Highest Bidder
Don't Ask for the Deposit Back

act no different than you feel
act no different than you feel
some will step away
others will sigh with relief
always remember nonmoral is not amoral
before you enter make a plow of
your hand to
test the air
they stamp your wrist to let you in
here's my stamp now leave me alone
pressing forehead to
wall gets ears seeing better
don't mention the wasp nest
they'll come with poison to
kill every one of them
we'll make peace with the nest
cooperation we learn on our own
at school it's only football and other war games
magpies eating entrails missing a face
it's all one cake for worms in the end
winter overlays a
white map toward
any direction
the night the kite came in on
no wind with no string
it was talking because
it was a talking kite
I'm Bob Kaufman and
Eileen Myles sent me
and he spoke no more
but hugged me
lots of hugs

My Orgone Box of Glass
Bottles Pillows and Music

hi it's me don't listen to them I didn't die
join me upright at
the singe marks where
the cremation didn't take
I hate coffee but I just survived so
let me have some tossed high in
the branches of the miracle
middle age could be 25
you just don't know
only love can
interrupt the
waiting
someone culled a file of people looking for you
don't be such a coward our research proves
you're a perfect match
pull muscle layer over skeleton
then skin
all the hearts are defective
it's a punishing road of sorrow
label says *try not to wilt in the sun*
each of us has gunpowder in a secret organ
my therapist says *learn to live with it*
I say *learn to fucking eradicate it*
my clairaudient friend these
ghosts are here for your ears
at this very moment
there are 54 million
people on Earth who
will die over the next

12 months
some of them
tonight
be careful out there

I Loved Earth Years Ago

I drew a map on you so I wouldn't get lost.
  – Doireann O'Malley

Dear Eileen, every night lately I dream about Mark, my boyfriend who renamed himself Earth back when he became an environmental and AIDS activist. I no longer call his death in Tennessee a murder, I call it an execution, executed for being queer!! It happened over a dozen years ago and few believed my story and the police told our mutual friends he killed himself. An execution not fit for police investigation, just another faggot punished for breaking God's laws in this good Christian nation. I will never apologize for my anger!! Delinquent Films is making a documentary about my new book and they questioned me about Earth. They also didn't believe me so they interviewed the sheriff who told them Earth was a suicide. THEN they talked with the coroner and HE corroborated every detail I've been saying for years. Earth was hogtied, gagged, tortured, covered in gasoline and burned to death. The coroner used the word *homicide* and said it's not possible this was a suicide.

I'm grateful *homicide* was said out loud, and that a film about my POEMS is the reason this investigation is FINALLY going to happen!! What does it take to get a faggot's execution investigated? POEMS!! The weight of poems has arrived!! I loved him so much, my gentle, sexy man, steward of flowers and worms. I'm going to be on a panel at the Ecopoetics conference in Berkeley with some of my favorite poets. I'm creating a (Soma)tic poetry exercise where I visit the places Earth and I loved. We had a garden plot in Philadelphia, but we also planted zinnias, marijuana, cucumber, kale, cowpeas, rosemary, lemon balm, and string beans along riverbanks and in overgrown, abandoned lots. The weight of poems is upon me, so I'm selling them for a little ruthless surrender. A decade is long enough to dream of revenge for a dead lover. For seven days I'll go to our favorite places for the poems. I'll also go on the internet to see what every ingredient I put into my body looked like when it was still growing. See fields of sesame plants while chewing their seeds, YES!!

He named himself Earth when planet extinction was clearest. He wanted to spend time in Tennessee and I warned him about country people. I was born and raised in rural Pennsylvania where everyone is proud of living in the country. I noticed at a young age that these PROUD COUNTRY people LOVE to poison, burn, shoot, and decapitate the natural world. Their pride is mostly invested in SUBDU-ING nature, always ready to prove who's Boss! It is difficult to tell them who they really are, like convincing my stupid father to STOP pouring ammonia and broken glass down the chipmunk holes. It is difficult to convince them of the harmless lives of tiny creatures who only need a few acorns and berries. I miss Earth. I loved him. I'm tired of being such a sad faggot but c'est la vie. His brutal execution is a mirror of every decision to pollute air, water, soil, lungs, hearts, communities of people, birds, fish, bears, stop, stop, STOP, STOP!! Are you hopeful we can stop in time? Let me write some poetry and try to calm down. Love you Eileen, and thanks for listening.

Ariana Reines Showed Me the World's First Guidebook Was a Twelfth-Century Pamphlet for Pilgrims

this is my refrigerator I won on
an American game show
once in a while I find myself
looking forward instead of back
hearing all dreamers talk at
once sends me into
the lower organs
I type your
name on the computer
delete it type it again
different each time
before I met you my
favorite color was
green light
now I serve poetry to
serve you
now I am famished for peace
now I watch a 90-year-old movie to
witness dead people talking singing
riding horses *samsara*
SAMSARA SAMSARA
I've been walking the border of sleep to find you
dreaming around the circumference of
a hole in the ground
the bravest thing sometimes is
how the morning is greeted
fight for the money or
fight for the soul the saying goes
but another goal is to
fight for neither
drip drip

drip the
soul of money
the loneliness of staying
too long in a
gentrified
neighborhood
tension of real
things that
seem unreal
a door left
open in the
skull as
a way out as
a tyranny to
let flow through the
wires in the wall
half the mind half the
morning kept a secret from
the cooling engine of
the dream
there is no
job harder than
setting eyes in
sockets to see right
most of your friends called you a
suicide my dear man
but I know the truth in
saying I will always
love you is a
currency worth
the length
of my

time
here
How to Ruin the Child is chapter one of
my new book *How to Ruin the Adult*

from Radar Reveries

Kingdom of the Coatimundi

For Michelle Tea & Ali Liebegott

I guess I should've closed my eyes when you
drove me to the place where your horses run free
  – Prince

In July 2012 I attended RADAR Lab writer's residency in Akumal, Quintana Roo, Mexico. For nine consecutive nights I prepared my crystal-infused-water dream therapy to help me remember my dreams. Each morning I would recall my dreams, then listen to a different PRINCE album in its entirety, DIRTY MIND, CONTRO-VERSY, PURPLE RAIN, etc., allowing the purple PRINCE landscape to reinvent the dreamscape. As soon as the album finished I would write for fifteen minutes, which was not so much a dream journal as it was a dream-lost-inside-PRINCE journal.

After breakfast I went down to the beach. Each morning from 9 a.m. to noon I would sit in the same place, one foot closer to the tide each morning. On the last day I sat directly in the tidal break with sturdy paper and a pen whose ink embeds into paper, a pen invented to prevent check fraud. PRINCE may wash my dreams away, but the ocean would not take my poems.

For a few minutes I would close my eyes to listen to the tide. Then I would sud-denly open my umbrella and stare at one of its polka dots, each one a different color of the spectrum. After staring at one polka dot for five minutes I would suddenly look out at the beach, coral reef, and ocean. The polka dot's color would show itself in the hue of a broken shell, or be found in the bow of a distant ship. One morning my eyes landed on the white of the umbrella, which is all the space surrounding the polka dots. I decided to go with it. When I tore the umbrella aside I noticed FOR THE FIRST TIME tiny white crabs who made their homes at the wettest part of the sand, continuously washed by the tide. The study of the crabs consumed my morning. One day I looked up from writing to see, a few feet from my face, a hundred yellow butterflies fluttering in a line down the beach above the surf. The parade of beauty kept me in awe: giant sea turtles, iguanas, and magnificent seabirds. One day I placed my large Lemurian crystal in the sand under the surf. RADAR Lab's amazing chef Christina Frank sat with me to witness the little silver fish surround the crystal. They LOVED IT! They would ride the surf to the crystal, surround it and KISS IT, ride the tide out, then ride it back in and KISS IT AGAIN!

From 3 p.m. to 6 p.m. I would sit in the bathtub to write. My favorite childhood liquid was FRESCA! I thought it went out of business, but it just moved to Mexico! I drank FRESCA all day long at the residency, and used it for the bathtub meditation, drinking mouthfuls, letting the grapefruit bubbles roil in my mouth while turning the shower on. I would touch the falling water with the tips of my fingers, then I would swallow the FRESCA and turn the water off. I would meditate on arguments from the archive of my unforgiving brain. Arguments I had, and arguments by others. Once I heard my mother and sister shouting in another room. My mother yelled, 'I SHOULD HAVE ABORTED YOU!' My sister yelled back, 'GRANDMOM SHOULD HAVE ABORTED YOU AND WE WOULD ALL BE FREE FROM THIS GODDAMNED MESS!' My mother BURST into tears, my sister left the room with a smile. She saw me and said, 'I TOLD HER!' I returned her smile and hugged her saying, 'YES you did my dear!' The MOMENT we embraced THE RELIEF of our grandmom's imaginary abortion WASHED OVER US BOTH! We laughed from so much pain and nonsense for a rolling tide. The brain holds all of our disasters in little, decrepit files marked and mismarked and repeating their vomitus sick, and sometimes a little too quiet from too much damage. These notes became nine poems, my homage to my mother who was not aborted, and to her children who were also not aborted.

Act Like a Painted Heart
Not a Painting of a Heart

nothing
beautiful
came again
there is no
thing worse
i have crawled
on my knees to
end its
dormancy
scalp as verb
everyone has
a favorite verb
but mores replace
mores replace mores
scalping your enemies makes
outstanding souvenirs
we elevated
a flower
or maybe
it lowered us
an extraordinary
effort to forgo
the souvenirs
soon enough we were told
never leave the kitchen
with this knife again
no matter who is
bullying you

Act Like Flower Pulling His Petals Out

let me know if
you need anything
i'm here to serve you
and just so you know
we're having a
sale on our
newest model it's
very nice it's where
your hand gets
held through the
difficult currents
later the
small ones
seem bigger
but our test
results show that
everyone who
hangs in there
winds up
ajar of their
former top
secret
desires
so please
let me know if
you need anything

Act Like Polka Dot on Minnie Mouse's Skirt

i am not a
family-friendly
faggot i tell
your children
about war
about their tedious future careers
all the taxes bankrolling a
racist tyrannical military
i'm the faggot at
dinner asking to
be alone
with the
children
tell them their
future happiness
depends entirely
on how well they
cultivate rebellion against
any structure that
does not hold their
autonomy and
creative intelligence as a priority
CHILDREN your bliss is at stake
CHILDREN listen carefully for the
lies your parents tell you
CHILDREN prepare for joy in ways
none of them will ever imagine
prepare to live with no regrets

While Standing in Line for Death

2013–2016

from Mount Monadnock Transmissions

For Prageeta Sharma

*Over a period of four centuries some nine million such hideous conflagrations
occurred, driving Europe's women out of power and their tribal traditions
completely underground. Sometimes to add to the horror and drive the lessons
home further, the bodies of strangled Gay men were stacked in with the kindling
at the witches' feet as 'faggots' of a new and horrible kind and as a sacrificial
symbol turned upon the people who had valued living faggots, sacred Gay men.*
  – Judy Grahn, from *Another Mother Tongue*

Yes poetry can handle this. This is the third ritual I did to overcome my depression
from my boyfriend Earth's murder. The third because the first two, while I liked the
resulting poems, left me feeling just as depressed, sometimes worse. The rituals
for creating poems have the power to change us in ways we have yet to fully explore, and I was determined to find the right ingredients for the ritual, and I did. It
worked.

Earth had moved to a rural queer community in Tennessee to work the gar-
dens, and he was happy the last time we talked on the phone, telling me about
budding trees and the delicious smells of spring. He told me about a cave he found
where he liked to meditate in the mornings. We made plans for me to visit and
spend the night together in the cave. We were excited. He told me to give Philadelphia his love.

Days after that phone call he was meditating in the cave when men bound and gagged him, tortured him, raped him, covered him in gasoline, and burned him alive. The police ruled his death a suicide. The sheriff told me to mind my own business every time I insisted Earth was murdered, and he called me Faggot like it was my name: he would say, 'Do you hear me Faggot?' Yeah, Faggot heard you. The police know who did it. Or they just don't care. Which is worse? My anger at the police and Earth's rapists and killers haunted my days. The coroner and paramedics, however, always called his death a homicide, which provided some comfort.

I am grateful to the MacDowell Colony for providing me with a little cabin in the woods for a couple of months to do this ritual in the shadow of Mount Monadnock. It was autumn and the leaves had started to fall. One of the ingredients of the ritual was to sit in the woods and focus on a distant tree trunk. Being patient, staring at the tree long enough, I would suddenly see every falling leaf at once. It can be as harrowing as it is cathartic to abruptly capture all motion with the eye, permitting the movement to sync up with an internal avalanche. I took notes for the poems. One night I dreamed I woke inside a tree, the wood surrounding me was a warm, fibrous silk and I could hear the sap moving inside a soft steady heartbeat.

The last time I saw Earth alive he gave me a clear quartz crystal he had carried in his pocket for over a year. After his death I put it away. It caused me pain with its psychic barbed wire; whenever I found it by accident my day would be ruined. When the first two rituals failed I knew I needed a more potent ingredient. I took Earth's crystal with me to the residency. This crystal had been on him every day for over a year doing what such crystals do, receive and store information. His breath and laughter, planting seeds in the dirt, his lips on mine, the way he tasted different in sunlight with snow, his inimitable warmth stored in the crystal's chambers. It was a little library of the man I loved.

Each morning I strapped Earth's crystal to my forehead, making certain it was pressed firmly against my third eye. Then I would swallow a smaller, round, clear quartz crystal. This was the worker-crystal whose job was to travel through my body, pulling the information out of Earth's crystal and flooding my bones, my tissue and blood, pumping his library through my heart and thoughts. Almost immediately my body calmed, every cell dropped its head back and sighed. The stress of loving a man murdered without justice lifted each day of the ritual toward peace. When I passed the small crystal into the toilet I would sterilize it and start over the next morning. I took notes for the poems.

I found my joy again beneath Mount Monadnock and I am thankful. We are time machines of water and flesh patterned for destruction, if we do not release the trauma. For years I had a movie playing in my head, my own little invention of torment, complete with a courtroom drama where Earth's still unknown rapists and killers were on trial. After a week of ritual the pernicious movie in my head faded and I immediately began taking better care of myself. From 1988 to 1998 I had been macrobiotic and athletic, the healthiest and happiest decade of my life. Earth's murder in 1998 and the additional violence of the police cover-up shook my confidence in this world and derailed me for years.

This ritual was my Restart Button. Today my love for Earth is healthier in a world that continues to kill faggots since the days when Christianity colonized pagan Europe, burning faggots with the witches, incinerating all they had to offer the world. 'Accelerant poured on victim and set afire,' the coroner wrote on Earth's death certificate.

The last time I saw poet Akilah Oliver before she died we were sitting at a bar after a poetry reading and I told her of the ritual I was about to do to overcome my depression over Earth's murder (not this ritual you are reading but the first one where I liked the resulting poem but felt no better). She was encouraging and we spoke of death as a shared space with all life, and this conversation led us down a dark thread about our planet's pillaged ecosystems. In a panic I said there was no way to fix our dying planet. She touched my shoulder and said, 'CA, you are about to do a ritual to heal yourself, and you are part of the planet so you are healing part of the planet by healing yourself.' It made us both smile and toast to healing the planet by healing ourselves. And today I hold a glass to let Akilah know that it worked finally, 'It worked Akilah, poetry did this to me and I am free!'

Of the 27 poems resulting from the notes taken during the ritual, 9 were from dreams while sleeping with Earth's crystal under my pillow. I call the poems 'Sharking of the Birdcage', and I am very happy they showed me the way back to my strength.

a spider's web is
made of digested
fly brains wings hairs
legs tears pheromones
attracting more flies
    dissolving us into the endeavor of love
      hold me to your song it is delicious
      hear you one more time in
        middle of night
        tooth it open
        love all unloved
        parts without pause
      Dear Ghost flickering with
      flames that no longer hurt
      deflated lungs expanding
        YOU SAY *They Can Only*
        Burn A Faggot Once

your murderers were the last
to touch you in this world
torpid song on repeat
pulled down the
rocky slope
I hold the shirt you left behind
the bottom was
visible before the descent
hours days months later
your shirt is gone
no I am wearing it
covered in cuts
layers of dust on my skin
still confident in gravity
still sliding down when
up now feels
too far
away

we threw our shoes across the garden
a promise from our feet to return
I throw dirt in the
other direction
hold roots
for tree to
comprehend eviction
ordered into   the colossal
where the bible is the hinge of law
drain river Jordan for
something new to perfect
get the Hillbilly jackpot if you
appear at correct location with
proper biblical
abomination
you win rape
torture
death
by fire

the men who killed you
justify your abbreviated breath
hold this bristling maw open
a place where I will
not allow infringements to proliferate
yelling *FUCK FORGIVENESS* in
my first revenge dream
punching their faces
harder then harder
smashing their
god-fearing
sense of
entitlement
licking blood
off my knuckles
I woke the
happiest faggot but
these days am happier
dreaming I'm holding you

when you died
the way you died
it was contaminating
a new danger of being lost and insecure
but reality can never be avoided forever
at the same moment who is afraid of whom
the killers or my beloved
or guilt of my continued song
desire is not what we achieve
it's a knife often carving the wrong way
or racking it in the alchemy of a mood
I should never trade youth for
poetry's resonance of aging
but I can put every poem
I ever wrote
in a pile
and burn
them if you
would appear
on the other side

the weight of a
poem on paper is
equal to its labor
for the verbose or
poets who prune
the words like me
did they love
any part of you when
asphyxiating your song
I lost a pen a book some money
feeling unexpectedly closer to you
I emptied closets bureaus cabinets
grated a carrot and refused to stop
did they love
anything at all when
covering you in gasoline
what would I not give
what would I not squander
to be your champion loser
how can it possibly be
how could they
light the match

your rapists were the last
to taste you in this world
their breath and
terror down
your neck
keeps me
up at night
but which
page of the bible says to
burn the faggot after
you force him to give
you your pleasure
each time I drink water dropped from clouds
water they burned out of your body I cup my
hands to catch you
in the revenge dream I behead one of them
spell your name on my face with his blood
the other is begging as I choke him
his neck as soft as your neck
I pull him off his knees
check for tattoos
is it him
is it you
I miss you
I love you

envelop crystal swallow crystal
thrust
crystal
up my
ass to
distract from
ten thousand worries
few things tire me more than
imagining
reincarnation
a child
struggling
all over again to
not favor war
not surrender to greed

the spirit of
your flowers is
my favorite shelter
we were in love is
the main
thing
faintest green light in
tree pulls me forward
whenever life is
beautiful makes
me think of you
carry color of the
forest to be with
you to belong to
this world with
you to have what
we have and that is it
yes the present
is between the
past and future
but is too radical
to be called
the middle

I still loved you after cutting down the trees
I still loved you as the car washed downstream
I still loved you after saying goodbye to the butterflies the elephants
I still loved you in a shard of light my finger in the web to

                              give it back tenfold
                              holding our
                              gorged fragment as
                              promised to
                              change if we
                              want change
                         another evening to
                              falter under
                              the chrysalis
              a wayward protein bloodletting from
              unforeseen orifice gathers us to
                   elongated grass-fed hours
                         falling victim to
                              the song in its
                              silken casing

know
thyself
except for a
small wild patch for the poems
waiting room played a T V cop
show from forty years ago
the murderer would be
out on parole now
erect with the
chaos of
our time
lingering
no more
over what to do
some places belong to
the way the dead were told to die
your naked back standing in moonlight chanting
I Prophesize I Prophesize I Prophesize I Prophesize

poetry or another
shovel working where
the real America buried you
the kind of men shown
a table with blueprints of
        our city to destroy us
    when they
punish us it is
exactly how we
  knew it would feel
 places with the least warmth
exchanged with
places we miss one another in
sunlight snorkel of corn silk as
 the hummingbird drinks your
wounds away
fuck the real
America up
the ass with
the fake one
    let it all be done you said
      let it all be done I said

another poet
apologizes at a microphone
weakening the hull of our ship
if you can't believe in your poems
leave them at home until you
learn to deserve them
this poem this poet
will not apologize
I'm tired of smelling my dead boyfriend
his swimming arms lost to my bed
it hurts to admit I love being alive
I broke and those pieces broke
and those pieces crushed to powder
things to avoid saying around me:
take it like a trooper
stiff upper lip
keep it together
don't let your mouth say these things
don't let your comfort be selfish cruelty
let them shriek
let them sob
don't be
a coward
about love

to talk me out of a sex change to
become a nun you argued that I just
gave a sex worker friend advice about
which hand to fist-fuck with to prevent fatigue
a crisp understanding in the shiniest branches
in life after death there is every
day harmony between my
feet and goals
clasp protein to cell
assembling a cloud
exchange a new
vowel for our
downpours
a generous
harvest of
flowers at back
of the throat you
laughed when I told
one of Philadelphia's
faggot-hating Nazis
If I can smell the
cheap whiskey
on your breath
there is no need to
ask if I'm listening

this is
exactly
the kind
of space
I want to
follow you into
holding your little
mute worm on a twig
make it marble
make it touch like tough winter
in the next life we will have longer love
better places with extended embraces
now we leave the song to return to the front
leaf closing on closeness of
mothers in the next world
overseeing premium
waste of the planet
reincarnate
anywhere
but here
land on a different rim

every
single
human
ambition
cultivated by
fear of death
it is not failure
but age you smell
I am often disgusted with
life here without you
despondence
growing sinister
the kind of fear when you
don't care if you
scrape the car while
leaving the parking lot
getting the fuck out before
the police arrive today we
give love that same
abandonment

Dear Earth it is okay to not
roll the stone back uphill
we rent memory storage in the world you
left behind
little wonder in this
dell of broken treaties
daisies bend under
our slightest breath
you did not answer
after you died
it is when
I learned
to be
lonely
everywhere
between dreaming and crying
until it calcified
and fell

it's awful without you making sound exist
sing for me I will sing for you
breathe and moan come on
what was it you wanted
us to think about after
you died you said
ponder this
but none of
us can
hear
it
please speak up
nothing now but a
medieval barking gargoyle
whoever gave you the tambourine
shall be sheriff of my tender zoo
I am not here
I am in the future
where I have always been
hurry back and forth
to kiss me my
ghost

You Don't Have What It Takes to Be My Nemesis

For Dorothea Lasky, who also puts up with a lot of assholes

To the friend you thought was a friend until they tried to sabotage a publishing opportunity. To the one who ripped your book in half on stage then wrote patronizing letters to the newspaper about how you should be writing and the poets you should be reading to become a real poet. HAHA!! To the creep who deleted your MP3 file because your reading was better than his. There are others, lying, conniving, envious sourpusses without the courage to be loyal to the love of friends and shared ideas. But finally to the worst of all, to the one you loved the most; your trusted collaborator, the one who wreaked true havoc, the gifted sociopath, the one you always dreaded, but they found you. That one, the best liar you ever met, who took a machete to your life, their drama akin to opera. Even still they are given the parting words, 'you don't have what it takes . . .'

Take notes about each of them for the poem, their names are unimportant as such cowards are rarely remembered. Create a line of tiny photographs of their faces on your computer, ALL IN A ROW, and then print it out; this will be the rolling paper for a cigarette. Cover their faces with equal amounts of the following dried ingredients: fennel seeds, pine needles, rose petals, mugwort, basil, white sage, red sandalwood powder, perique tobacco, and marijuana. These ingredients quell negative thoughts, shift gears for transformation, and also invoke prophetic dreams, clairvoyance, happiness, honesty, peace of mind; and marijuana because you put up with a lot of shit and deserve to enjoy yourself! Roll it up, keep track of which enemy you are smoking, but smoke them all, SMOKE THEM ALL, sucking their faces into your lungs while writing notes for the poem, notes about the ones who didn't have what it takes to beat you down, the ones who never deserved your friendship in the first place. Exhaling their faces on a braid of smoke is more satisfying than the usual forms of forgiveness. Find your poem in the notes and utterly relish your day!

PS: In the foreword to the extraordinary book *The Grasshopper's Man* by Rosalie Moore, chosen by W. H. Auden for the 1949 Yale Series of Younger Poets, Auden writes, 'Poetry flourishes when the opponents are determined and evenly matched but, if any party gains too complete a victory and succeeds in suppressing its rivals, poetry invariably declines.'

I Feel So Lonely When You Touch Me

like most people
ghosts want
listeners
inquiring gender of
tree quaking in shade
rips your collar to
pieces we meet
ourselves whole
at same time
order of the
way some will
ruin themselves
gentleness thrust
into a clean glass
ideate YES angling a wider indulgence
you and your
broken pencil
write *it's a*
writing world
but do get
on with it
listen to
blood
of trees
imbuing
interest rate
with sunshine
suffering passed to
a hired hand

Power Sissy Intervention #1: Queer Bubbles

For Candice Lin

I hate the word homophobia. It's not a phobia. You are not scared. You are an asshole.
  – frequently misattributed to Morgan Freeman

I occupied a busy street corner in Asheville, North Carolina, to bless children with bubbles that will make them queer. Not gay and lesbian, but QUEER! Bubbles of course do not have such powers, bubbles have only the power to be bubbles, and some parents knew that and thought the whole thing was funny and would say, 'That's cool, I will love my children no matter what.' I took notes for the poem.

But MOST parents were not happy about Queer Bubbles at all: 'Ooo bubbles, look at the bubbles sweetheart, look at the pretty bubbles.' I would blow bubbles for their little hands and say, 'These bubbles will assure that your child will grow up to be a healthy, happy, revolutionary Queer who will help rid the world of homophobia, misogyny, racism, and other forms of stupidity.' Parents pulled away nervously saying, 'Sorry, sorry.' One mother abruptly yanked her blond son's hand, 'C'mon honey ice cream, ice cream!' The boy cried, reaching for the bubbles as she refused to look in my direction, pulling him from the queering of the bubbles. Most parents though just said, 'Sorry, I'm sorry,' as they walked away. I took notes for the poem.

The fear of queer will not dissolve with sorry, the apology is not acceptable, especially if their children grow up to be queer. Asheville purports to be a liberal, laid-back city, but Queer Bubbles pulled the veil aside for a closer look. One man said, 'Jesus loves you.' I said, 'I don't think so.' His face screwed up and he yelled, 'YES HE DOES!' Jesus loves the queers, isn't that nice? And his angry messenger roams the street to tell us so. WE MUST INSIST that a redistribution of wealth always include The Love. How can we be there for one another? How can we be assured that everyone gets The Love? Notes from the ritual became a poem.

Every Feel Unfurl

                                      I was naked
                               on a mountaintop
                               kissing someone
                               who loved me
                               people fully
                               clothed 9
                               thousand
                                      feet
                                      below
        as crossed out as this cage I
        say I belong to no more
        the stars let me off the hook again
                      this is so new I don't get it
                      hear   myself sing with
                         a voice I do not recognize
                      the best voice to happen to
                            me I want it back
                                  each night
          there is nothing little about little lights in the sky
                      now the pronunciation is perfect for another
                      morning of lips performing their duty to verb
                      shrouding ourselves by light of
                      damage control stations of rhetoric
                      lips as piglet prepared to
          be hacked apart beneath a greenery of
      mansions a mess the ambulance cannot reach
   there is nothing little about the cicada revving up while
                                  we think our car horns
                                  are so impressive

My Faggot Kansas Blood Confessions to the Earth

For Anne Boyer

In a Kansas field I spent several hours burying my feet in the soil while listening to the insects, birds, and cars on the highway beyond the trees. I was born January 1, 1966, at the 838th Tactical Hospital, Forbes Air Force Base of Topeka, Kansas. My mother said the doctor held me by my ankles and announced, 'ANOTHER FINE SOLDIER FOR JESUS!' And I say FUCK YOU to those first words said to me! My mother ate food grown on this land when I was inside her, we drank from the same aquifer; the sky was as big as it is today. I took notes for the poem. I dug a hole and deposited shit, piss, vomit, blood, phlegm, hair, skin, fingernails, semen, and tears, and in that order. I apologized for being alive.

I apologized for having no answers on how to stop the hyper-militarized racist police on the streets of America while the racist US military is on the streets of Arab nations. I apologized for paying taxes that purchase the bullets, bombs, and drones. I apologized for not convincing my queer sisters and brothers that repealing Don't Ask, Don't Tell was only putting a sympathetic face on a multitrillion-dollar military-industrial complex. I apologized for not finding a way to protect Chelsea Manning. I apologized for many things for a long while then covered the hole holding my offerings and took more notes for my poem.

My Faggot Blood on His Fist

the first time
someone sent
Homer through
the internet
        dot
    dot   dot
    we are all
        falling in
    love while
    standing in
line for death
    fuck this way we
    slowly adjust to suffering
    an ant finding her way home in
    the downpour
    lovers are weapons subjugating your
    heart if you smell them years after they die
            if you feel
            destroyed
            let us talk
        do not
            turn it
            off yet
        we dreamed
            our obliteration for
            centuries then
            Hollywood said
This is what it will look like
Or maybe this Or maybe this
you think it's everyone's job to
make you feel good which
        is why we all hate you

the disgraced hairdresser
pours us another shot
we will figure
it out my friend
the ocean is
never far
when you feel
your pulse

Monkey Grass

For Divya Victor

The animals of the world exist for their own reasons. They were not made for humans any more than black people were made for whites or women for men.
– Alice Walker

Before visiting Nanyang Technological University (NTU) in Singapore I visited monkeys at the Philadelphia Zoo (Prison). It is very difficult to witness pitiless, unenlightened parents normalize (even CELEBRATE) for their children the incarceration of innocent animals. In this ritual I carried in my left hand a small piece of celestite with 9 blades of grass plucked outside the zoo (prison). Celestite's name is derived from the Latin meaning 'of the sky', and it works on opening our top three chakras: Throat, Third Eye, and Crown. It was important I chose a stone that was capable of absorbing any communications as a temporary battery and transmitter without the complications of my needing to translate the messages for myself, since the messages were not for me. It was up to the wild monkeys of Singapore to interpret our unfortunate cousins' stories from the United States.

I clenched the crystal and grass while making eye contact with Colombian black spider monkeys, and white-bellied spider monkeys. Their faces were anxious and sad. The Colombian government was not demanding the release and return of one of their nation's most beautiful natural gifts, and the monkeys knew it. The animals' depression did not seem to register with parents and children pointing and laughing, eating candy and enjoying their freedom. I did not care that they occasionally stared at me as I spoke out loud to the monkeys, telling them that I am on my way to visit our cousins in Singapore where they swing freely in the trees. 'What would you like me to tell them?' I stared into their eyes and said, 'I love you little cousins,' then left the zoo (prison), putting the crystal and grass blades in my left pocket. I took notes for the poem before, during, and after the zoo (prison) visiting hours.

When you know something is wrong in the world you must confront it. Be sad, be angry, be active, and never apologize, ever! A couple of years ago someone overheard me saying, 'Zoos are prisons where not a single prisoner has ever seen a lawyer!' This person said, and this is a verbatim quote, 'But animals really are better off in zoos. It's safer for them.' And so began one of the stupidest conversations of my life, and no matter what I said this person was confident that imprisonment was the best choice for animals. 'It's a dangerous world out there,' they informed me. I tapped the side of my head and said, 'It is not nearly as dangerous as the world IN HERE this evening!' Conversations such as this one are exactly why I prefer all other animals over human beings! I LOATHE my species for the overwhelming lack of empathy for any creature other than our own! In the mid-1990s there was a fire in the ape house at the Philadelphia Zoo (Prison) – 23 sentient beings died that day. It was shocking, and when the news reporter said, 'Luckily no one was injured,' I called the station to complain: 'You mean NO HUMANS were injured! How can you say 23 died but no one was injured?'

The eyes of the captive monkeys haunted me and I touched the outside of my pocket where I kept the crystal and grass. After I arrived in Singapore I asked my friend Divya whether there were any wild monkeys in the area and was excited to hear that her husband Josh had an ongoing encounter with a wild monkey on the NTU campus. My eyes constantly scanned trees and lawns. One day, after teaching a poetry workshop I walked from the building to find a small group of people photographing themselves with something in the background. When I craned my neck I was excited to see two brown monkeys hugging each other near the pond. All my life I had wanted to see monkeys who are FREE. I sat in the grass and threw several pieces of fruit to them. One of the creatures came over, then the other, eating delicious melon slices, their eyes and demeanor completely different from our enslaved cousins'. I placed the crystal and grass on the ground between us with a last melon slice. When one monkey touched the crystal under the melon she LOOKED at me suddenly and ran away, agitated. I admit feeling guilty for causing her anxiety with the message from our enslaved cousins, but the other monkey hugged her and comforted her. I took notes for the poem as they groomed each other and ran across the grass, their movements and play shaking off the humiliation and degradation of our cousins in Philadelphia.

It was one of the most exciting times of my life with nonhuman creatures. I was high with joy for the rest of the day. Then after cooking dinner I turned on Channel NewsAsia and sat with my bowl of rice and beans. I went from being joyful to being completely shocked when a report aired from a busy street in Japan where a chimpanzee named Chacha was on an electric pole after escaping from the zoo. Chacha had broken out of prison! And at first I was excited. It felt like a message. It was a surreal coincidence. How could this be? Then a man shot a tranquilizer dart into Chacha's shoulder and the beautiful animal who had looked happy to be out in the world felt immediate and intense pain. Chacha SCREAMED at the man, then grew limp and fell to the outstretched net waiting below. Humans wrapped Chacha in a blanket and put him in a van and drove him back to prison for the rest of his life on this human-dominated planet. Why do we cage animals? Because we can! Because they are weaker and we do not mind exploiting this weakness and sharing our authority over them with our children on a Sunday afternoon. It is also more efficient to gather all the animals and put them in cages in one place near our homes rather than fly all over the globe to see them. Efficiency breeds brutality every single time. Chacha, my heart breaks for you and I want to visit you one day in the zoo (prison) and tell you that I love you but have no idea how to save you. I unexpectedly took even more notes for the poem – the darkest of the day's notes – and watched the rebroadcast later in the evening to take more notes as Chacha screamed and fell from freedom all over again.

The way we mistreat animals is evidence we are far from being able to rescue our own lives at this point. We need to start spreading compassion. Can we begin today, please? I am asking this to myself, and passing it along.

This Is Not the Master It Is the Lost Visitor

sky
linking skin
the moon heaves
tide of tears in a new direction
potted flower sitting
on other side of
war intact
rereading my first poetry notebook
excitement of surrendering
to the spirits is
what remains
looking and listening
with the dead who
unlace my syntax
cooked to the bone
a copy of the poem for the defense
another for the prosecution
aiding and abetting my
absorption of more
than the allowable
amount of light
borders spirits have told me
are flesh in every way to be
transgressed as
champion and
traitor alike

from Marfa Poetry Machine in 36 Rituals

For Jason Dodge

God has been replaced, as he has all over the West, with respectability and air conditioning. – Amiri Baraka

The Lannan Foundation presented me with a generous fellowship to live and write in beautiful Marfa, Texas, for two months. My working-class mother thinks I have pulled off a bank heist rather than believe anyone would be foolish enough to pay me to write my poems. I said, 'I know, Mom, I know. It is amazing with all the love our country gives to war and genocide that there is any left over for a poet!' I did 36 rituals a day for 36 days, taking notes between each ritual, the notes harvested later for the poems. Here is a list of the rituals I did each day to create the Marfa Poetry Machine:

1: Sage Poets
Burn sage to honor a different living poet each morning, saying the poet's name out loud while wearing a ceramic hamsa the poet Erica Kaufman gave me. 'This morning as every morning with poetry as my strength, I honor the poet _____.'

2: Crystal Supplement
Place the day's food in a glass bowl surrounded by crystals that have been programmed to boost cell proliferation and heighten organic vibrational patterns for

greater nutritional gain. The steady pulse of crystal frequencies saturating plants, beans, and grains.

3: Reiki Sunrise Before Sunrise
Watch sunrise on Edgar Cayce Institute Meditation Room webcam in Virginia Beach while giving Reiki to myself, preparing for the sun's arrival in Texas.

4: Reiki Sunrise
An hour later watch sunrise on porch while giving myself Reiki. Setting my day by the sun plugs me into a natural clock.

(I will have two sunrises a day with two time zones: one online in Virginia Beach, another in Texas. But only one sunset, to cheat the grave.)

5: Yoko Molecular Infusion
While cooking breakfast play the album *RISING* by Yoko Ono next to the stove, her music finding its way into the fiber of the food as she sings, 'Listen to your heart, respect your intuition, make your manifestation, there is no limitation, have courage, have rage, we're all together.'

6: Cell Knitting
Chew each mouthful of breakfast 36 times, meditating on food cells becoming my own cells of Yoko-Crystal infusion.

7: Elvis Penetrating Crystal
Meditate on a postage stamp of Elvis Presley (a gift from friend Jenn McCreary) through a clear shaft of flawless citrine, the guardian gemstone of manifestation.

8: Elvis Blackout
Wearing headphones sitting inside a closet with door closed listening to the length of a different Elvis song each day then as it finishes taking notes by flashlight.

9: Marfa Gratitude
Standing in front of the house on Summer Street taking a slow 360-degree view, grateful for the people who make Marfa what it is. You can surround yourself with

the best art in the world, but what actually makes a town is its citizens, and Marfa is home to some of the most thoughtful people I have ever met.

10: Log Bench Visualization

Sit on log bench in Summer Street Park. Gaze at the landscape without blinking. Close eyes and remember what was seen. Open eyes and look for what was missed. With each day the landscape grows more complete inside me. Later while falling asleep I visualize the park, recalling the details clearer and clearer throughout the 36 days.

11: Giant Installments

Watch five-and-a-half minutes of the movie *Giant* (1956), filmed in Marfa and starring Elizabeth Taylor, Rock Hudson, and James Dean. (Five-and-a-half-minutes times 36 is the length of the film.) 'Bick, you shoulda shot that fella a long time ago. Now he's too rich to kill.' (A line of Uncle Bawley's.)

12: Intersecting Temperatures

Outside the Pueblo Market focus on a color in the parking lot, buildings, or the sky: a yellow car or a bit of pink gum or an orange cat. Then walk the market aisles to find the same color on cans and other packaging and read the list of ingredients, like on a can of peas, as if it were the legend to a map. And ask the label out loud, 'HOW are these peas showing the way out of darkness to the sanctioned interior?'

13: Sentinel Pine

All my life I have made friends with trees. I take my magnifying glass to study the giant pine growing behind an abandoned building near Pueblo Market. She is tall and old and Donald Judd must have taken notice of her perfect symmetry of branches holding herself in spaces of green and brown, her angelic exhale of crown. There was an ant and I think she was the same ant, there most days crawling up the narrow ravines of bark. I dabbed on the bark a little brown rice syrup, always eaten, always relished.

14: Aphrodite's Element
Place pennies on railroad tracks next to the post office. Copper is the metal of Aphrodite – the goddess of Love – and we must not forget this, ever, that copper is her element on Earth. Find flattened pennies from the day before and leave them on the sidewalk, squashed heads up.

15: Regret-Reversal Spell
Close eyes and think of an embarrassment from the past. Imagine the former self in the middle of the situation shrugging and laughing.

16: We Are All Cogs of a Beautiful Machine
Find one natural item a day – a twig, little stone, feather, a bit of fluff on a breeze – and wind it, twist it into my longest strands of hair. Leave it tangled in my hair while writing, then untangle it.

17: Cogs of a Marfa Poetry Machine
Arrange found natural items on back porch, a growing machine.

18: Page 36
Read page 36 of different books written by former Lannan Fellows. For instance, 'Expunging Palestinians politically or physically from Israel's body politic is an idea with broad support within the admittedly narrow Zionist political spectrum' (from Ali Abunimah's *The Battle for Justice in Palestine*, from Haymarket Books).

19: Yoko Molecular Infusion Part Two
While cooking supper play next to the stove the 2007 album *Yes, I'm a Witch* by Yoko Ono, her music finding its way into the fiber of the food as she sings, 'Yes, I'm a witch, I'm a bitch, I don't care what you say, my voice is real, my voice is truth, I don't fit in your ways . . . Each time we don't say what we want to say we're dying.'

20: Cell Knitting Part Two
Chew each mouthful of my supper 36 times, meditating on food cells becoming my own cells of Yoko-Crystal infusion.

21: Reiki Sunset
Watch sunset over the desert at end of Third Street while giving myself Reiki.

22: Lost Horse
Have one shot of Jack Daniel's at the Lost Horse Saloon so as to meet people and enjoy this space where one night a woman rode a beautiful white horse INTO THE BAR! (Ask Tim Johnson at the Marfa Book Company if you don't believe me.) The lost horse always finds its way.

23: Marfa Lights
Look for the Marfa Lights at the viewing station on Route 90. Every night I saw them: sometimes as balls of white light rising from the earth, other nights riding the air sideways and changing colors. Someone told me they were reflected car lights. I said, 'Oh really, then what were they in 1888 and earlier, long before the metal horse arrived in Marfa?'

24: For the Architects We Live With
Each night I play the recording *Duet for Pen & Pencil*, composed by Christine Olejniczak. Then I walk from room to room with a flashlight to study this house designed by architect Kristin Bonkemeyer. I pause in each room to imagine her original blueprints of the building and say out loud, 'THIS is where I write in Kristin's drawing, THIS is where I play music in Kristin's drawing; THIS is where I cook, eat, and this is where I dream in Kristin's drawing.'

25: Peccary Vigil
Sit quietly on front porch hoping to spot the tribe of javelinas who like to eat the prickly pear cactus in the yard. Several nights THERE THEY WERE, little chattering tusks, hairy, stinky, and glorious to behold.

26: Sage Poets Part Two
Burn sage to honor a deceased poet each evening. 'This evening as every evening with poetry as my strength, I honor the poet _____.' For instance, R.I.P. Amiri Baraka, who died the first week I was in Marfa.

I was raised by people who spent their lives working in factories where they were treated like bad children who needed to be disciplined for demanding health care and a liveable wage. They formed unions to combat the company, with local, state, and federal governments poised against them. I did these 36 rituals for them. Freedom, poetry, and Love for them. Amiri Baraka said, 'A man is either free or he is not. There cannot be any apprenticeship for freedom.' The resulting 36 poems are a poetic measurement titled *Width of a Witch*.

Mercury.1

an admirer for

every odor crawling

with

light overhead

when something is ON it

wills itself to take the space

following great fishing maps

flailing mostly in the middle

a poem about

love wakes

everyone from port to starboard

a complete surrender to injuries of affection

it's the breaking point just about every day around here

we fix an

inside-out thing

but it was fine and   now it is inside out

Venus.1

poets the sentient seismographs
but only other poets are listening
we are the new   CASSANDRA
vibrating in middle of a
Cy Twombly painting
you moaned
showing me the
face inside the
face on the coin
yes my dear but I never
sleep with poets
then we kissed
then we stopped talking
poets getting naked not talking
pushing the miracle
poets screwing harder and fighting harder
magnifying the maw of our abyss

Home.2

I love walking on flat surfaces
if mountains
were flat I
would climb
them all
a shot of   gold in the seam
grafted from grown children of the gods
we are ordered to
believe them
cocks shoved into
mellow afterthoughts
clammy groaning magic
turtle meat with little
hat and dress come
see my little baby
gather around
my little baby
pushing her carriage up
the flat mountain
down to the
top

Jupiter.1

as backup
money became
IOUs my lipstick
smear gave cheating
a certain charm
just kiss me
asshole
nothing like
screaming to give the theater of sex away
the last one was the last one
until the new last one comes winging in
it's poetry it's always about love
snake oil salesman in bathtub
pennies on his eyelids
when his spirit   gets
caught on teeth of
the pumpkin we stick
a candle inside

Jupiter.2

he punched my face to remind me
    of something I forgot
  he apologized when he
  stopped hating faggots
congratulations I am remembering
all   of it now
all night egging him on to jump higher and higher and
this is not the way he wanted things to make up the rest of the road
                never mind me telling him it is over
                    that
                    all we
                    came
                    up here for was the love

Jupiter.3

can I babysit
teach them
basic disobedience
to be deaf to factory bells
there's an annoying poet
who says she killed poetry
just ask her at each poetry   reading
'is this another memorial service for you'
if poetry is dead call me a necrophiliac
I don't want children to inherit the earth
I want them to snatch it from heedless
adults before it's milked
all wish lists at
once is
heavenly

Jupiter.4

'I'm sorry I'm dying'
I couldn't believe he said it
I can't believe I held his hand
and didn't ask him why he said it
they leave the sobbing to the survivors
a very
nasty
trick
like idiots we accept
centuries of anger through our pens
it's okay to be happy is what
you have been waiting to hear as
you approach the room where
I just   wrote in red NO

Saturn.1

butterfly on a tissue box
not a real one
a painting
a monarch
one more sign
for anguish
poured and
poured a choice to feel or
stack bricks
between
I was sad when my
talented friend started designing
television   commercials
he told me to grow up
but the rocks in the desert I touch
signal an endless new place something
without money saying 'never tire of
demanding love for the world'

Saturn.2

I thought the radio
sang 'return to the sky'
I wasn't even close to
the song or the sky
I am looking for a place to
dump my enemies
not their bodies
their   grief
the deepest body of water
is not hopeful in the desert
I hold a microphone to the ants pouring from their hole
I thought they sang 'return to the sky return to the sky'
not even close

Saturn.3

you wanted to die
you told me to shut up
it was up to me to ignore you
to keep talking
my poem was
wrong about death
about that
about   it
turn out the lights to
hear ourselves think
squeezing my hand
a little too hard you are squeezing yourself back to life
I don't complain
let the spider decide for the spider
which lets the spider decide for the fly

Neptune.4

no one knows where I am in the morning and I like that
set my periscope on breath of dreaming tyrants
heir to a forest
do you mean fortune
no I mean forest caressing wound of earth surrounding it
twelve trees is a forest these days
clinging to dirt between
shopping malls   and banks
everything gets caught clinging between
shopping malls and banks
ask your children
what the new
moon requires

Pluto.1

the pearl starts over
a new grain of sand
we are going to find
in the planet of blue
a freshly written eviction note
gone fishing for better tenants
a sash hanging off the horse
told the story   without you
the kind of children we deserve who rob us in our sleep
we never need to believe in anything again
they take our car and money and head for the beach

Cremation Cocktail

For Jeremy Halinen

The Book of Frank makes me happy. I come from a poor, mostly illiterate rural American community where none of the houses of friends, family, or neighbors had bookshelves. It humbles and amazes me to come from such an environment and have a book I wrote translated into half a dozen languages. Over a period of 18 years I wrote this work, making 1,584 poems in total. Black Mountain College poet and publisher Jonathan Williams was originally going to publish the book through his Jargon Society press. I was incredibly honored and would go to his home in North Carolina to work on the manuscript with Jonathan and my friend Jeremy Halinen, who was the Jargon intern at the time. Except for me, they are the only other people to have read all 1,584 pages.

I miss Jonathan. Miss the endless supply of poets whose work he introduced me to, like Merle Hoyleman and Mary Butts, the kinds of writers who turn you around, lighting your way with their genius. He died around the spring equinox. I was walking with a group of friends to a bar in Philadelphia after a poetry reading when someone read us a text that Jonathan had just died, jackknifing the evening to sorrow. The bar was packed and the music loud, but we found a booth. After we toasted to the long and adventurous life of Jonathan Williams someone asked what was going to happen to my book now that he was gone. I said I didn't want to think about it, and that is when on the other side of the bar an old man stood up and started to shove people out of his way, walking toward our booth, a man who never bathed and who mumbled to himself. A friend was sitting across from me who had worked at the bar for many years and said no one had ever heard a full sentence from his mouth, and his odor kept everyone at bay.

He plowed his way through the noisy crowd and stopped at our booth, staring at me for an uncomfortable minute. Then he said this same sentence a dozen times, 'Don't worry, we have it taken care of, it will be better than you can imagine, we're looking out for you.' Then he said, 'You are my little princess,' and kissed the top of my head, then plowed the way back to his barstool on the other side of the bar. We were amazed! Jonathan Williams did that! He wanted to tell me this information to put me at ease about the book we had worked so hard on together, but he needed someone in the room who was so far removed from normalized, respectable behavior that he could walk his spirit inside them and have them speak on his behalf. The man had said the sentence over and over, his inflection exactly the same each time as if a recording had been placed in his head. Knowing Jonathan's temperament I can only imagine he was annoyed when the man repeated it too much and interrupted him with the little princess and kiss salutation. A week later I saw him again but he did not see me. The man who had said this incredibly comforting sentence to me and then kissed the top of my head calling me his little princess did not see me, just walked past me on the sidewalk.

Soon afterward the manuscript won the Gil Ott Book Award, chosen by Nathaniel Mackey, Myung Mi Kim, Eli Goldblatt, and Charles Alexander, and was published by Chax Press. Wave Books later published Frank where he continues to live happily today. I am grateful to all of the many dedicated people at these presses and to my poetry hero Eileen Myles, who wrote the afterword to the Wave edition. The book contains 130 poems, the only pages from the box of 1,584 poems that were published. For years I have been asked to consider a sequel or to enlarge the book, and I would sit with the box and consider it, but in the end I prefer the selections I made with Jonathan and Jeremy. The Wave edition is how I want the length and depravity of Frank's life measured.

Poetry is a window into the magic of this world that never once asked me to apologize. Poetry took me out of the soul-crushing factory town of my childhood, revealing itself to be a source of autonomy that once grabbed by its horns utterly transfigures our lives if we refuse to let go, and I will not take this force for granted. To honor that space is to have our poems be exactly the way we want them in the world. I read the box of poems out loud, all 1,584 pages of them, then placed a small, smooth piece of rose quartz crystal on top of the stack of paper and lit them on fire, watching them burn.

Afterward I swallowed the crystal; it tasted like smoked blood. The pile of ashes was remarkably small for 18 years of writing, and that was humbling as I gathered them in my cupped hands and mixed them into a warm bath with jasmine flowers. In the bath I massaged the ash and jasmine into every inch of my body, and took occasional drinks of the cremation cocktail to join the crystal working its way through my digestive organs. During the ritual I took notes that became a poem titled 'There Is No Prison Named Love.'

PS: Edgar Cayce and Jack Spicer both understood that poets are recording whispers from the spirit world with our poems. Witnessing Jonathan Williams walk inside the man to have him relay his message was a gift, watching the recently deceased poet flex his new spirit body. 'We' are looking out for you he said, the 'we' meaning Jonathan and my other spirit guides? I am most appreciative to Jonathan for his kindness to me in life and after life.

There Is No Prison Named Love

your dogs
have my scent
I will never allow you to
stain my eyes with your
angels and martyrs
I no longer lie still to
let you sob into my open mouth
I'm not here for conversion old man
I'm here to bury you with your dogs
all it takes is an airplane in my mind and
you are gone you get it
how you must suffer
pretending to be kind
like the days when
codependence was what
everyone dreamed they wanted
I fixed the broken leg of
poetry the only
influence that
never tried to
restrain me
for my help
poetry put
a light
under
my rib
moths follow as
we stroll into
the night

Amanda Paradise:
Resurrect Extinct Vibration

2016–2020

Golden in the Morning Crane Our Necks

in a past life I was
a little fish who
cleaned the
shells of
turtles
a dream
helped me
remember their
deep voice of thanks
many nights I heard sharks waiting
for the tide to draw me near
when the calendar runs out
it feels lucky another awaits
all I have ever wanted was to
forge the English language into
a spear and drive it into my heart
between leaping and being shoved
no lonelier place to put my faith for the
swinging motion inside the dance we share
don the extraordinary suit for this ordinary day
take our time studying trees to imagine the
nests we would build if we were birds
I ask all
you talented
people spending
many creative hours
perfecting killer drones
guns and bombs to please
know we are waiting for
you on the other side
of art in the No
Kill Zone

On All Fours I Am a Seat for the Wind

most of my family's
international travel
is being sent to war
if we judge love we
can kill off anything
dragged by our hair
across the days until
they make their way
inside our dreams where we get to evict them
I want to thank the one who invented knocking on the door
but no one remembers their name to tattoo across my knuckles
I asked an archaeologist about first time she stuck a shovel in the ground
her answer had same restorative powers as the gravedigger's
when we die we can no longer wipe the muck off
just lie there becoming shit of the world
eat a chip of your own dried blood
join me in the cannibal sunshine
fully persuaded by the
world through song
each morning a blue
jay screams at edge
of the clear-cut forest
I scream with her at
the bleeding stumps
scream inside something
borrowed like ocean like skin
I want to see before I die a
mink wearing a human scarf
skin from a handsome
hairy leg
MEOW

Acclimating to Discomfort of the System Breaking Beneath Us

I do not take any
calls except from
the century we are in
when there is no bible in my hotel room
it makes me sad to have no place to put
my filthy poems for future guests
it is important to let them know
everyone should burn with abandon as soon as the heat is available
be a self-styled alarm clock no one can shut off
be the storm Love places in someone's home
are you sure we can handle this
because I am absolutely certain
c'mon wind knock us around
we are a tide that cures ills
look at us in the mirror
as soon as the invented language enters
us something else will vibrate in our skin
opening door with teeth of the future to
the place where we let the freer feeling go
when you told me you had been looking for me
we pressed through every
invisible barrier between us
I watched you gently let the gods
know you are ready to win the lottery
there were people from the
19th century alive in my
lifetime many years ago
I met some of them
they are all gone now
as we hold on to
the side of one
another howling down
the velocity of seconds

900 Chocolate Hearts a Minute at the Candy Factory

estimate number of
near-misses after
interrupting the
angel prying your
father's jaws apart
fashioned on tip of a fork
car horn at door to the birth canal
living section of dawn cooking inside the poet
today is the day we reject this vexing sell-by-date worry
no guarantee we will cohere in our broken patch of garden
when you look at me you see
mostly water who will
one day hasten to
join a cloud
a thing I know for
certain is to cook
companionship into
food to taste and
become fellowship
eat a leaf with a hole
to share nourishment
with a future butterfly
you believe in sharing
at least you used to
I know you want
to shock me with
reports of enjoying
gloryholes and I can
act shocked to amuse
you yet I wonder if you
ever look up to the wall
thinking it will be his eyes

Auguries Cast Aside

to enter the sky with our bodies
the principal concern for
inventing airplanes
no one taught me this
any more than they taught me
to say good morning to my hippocampus
but I do because I love my hippocampus
I was in a band one summer
we never could harmonize
we smiled and kept playing
we loved our united disunity
a frantic enraptured focus
chewing its way out
how awkward the
archer after
shooting
his arrow
remembering
first time getting
into bed just
for sex
they say
I'm old now
ask my advice
all I have to offer is
make as many mistakes as
you can handle but make them
as soon as possible and please do
not waste time following each other
from opposite sides of the river
when storm blows wig off

my head it simply means
it is time to let the
storm take
its share

Only in Stacking Books Can the
Tree Feel Its Weight Again

I am so fucking sick of nations
and the men who love them
the number of suicides
this afternoon hiding
in bottom of a cup
I feel feral out here
found a man who likes me like that
found a man who lives the way I do
7 years on the road anniversary soon
you only have to destroy
yourself for love until it is normal
which makes love normal
and refuse to live a day without it
an inferno of it
at 16 sleeping with
my mother's boyfriend
I was overwhelmed with it
solids form around you until you
struggle no more beneath it
feel throat open in a word
naming new stars moving across
the ceiling from the disco ball
constellations with stories to
soften hardened hearts
we finish the night
reading poetry out loud
last night Erica Kaufman's
mind-blowing *Post Classic*
poetry and love
sure know how to

hang a Welcome sign out
measure and transmit from
the pink and adorable telemetry
no more waiting between parentheses
we now excel in the ether while holding hands

Memories of Why I Stopped Being a Man

For Jason Dodge

it's normal
if your cock
gets hard while
you are shooting
my uncle told me
on my first deer hunt
Pythagoras knew the music
of Jupiter and Mercury
long before NASA
but to begin again
no hero itching
at the door
that never-ending search for weakness in
neighbors siblings coworkers rival football teams
after seeing the open body of muscle and blood
we had horrible ideas about what to do with our lives
imagine how they gathered around the first
cannon ever fired sweaty excited rock hard
before he died Kalashnikov confessed
to suffering unbearable nightmares
surrender your nouns to my verbs
he said he said he said he said
in a game of Russian roulette
I won a pair of glasses
that can see the wind
I walk around town each night watching the
slightest breeze approach dry leaves like a premonition
after a million years of dreaming
the solution is still the same
hold me to your bruised song
until it warms me right

Glitter in My Wounds

first and most important
dream our missing friends forward
burn their reflections into empty chairs
we are less bound by time than the clock maker fears
this morning all I want is to follow where the stone angels point
birdsong lashing me to tears
heterosexuals need to see our suffering
the violent deaths of our friends and lovers
to know glitter on a queer is not to dazzle but to
unsettle the foundation of this murderous culture
defiant weeds smashing up through cement
you think Oscar Wilde was funny
well Darling I think he was busy
distracting straight people
so they would not kill him
if you knew how many times I
have been told *you're not like my*
gay best friend who tells me
jokes and makes me laugh
no I sure as fuck am not
I have no room in my life to
audition for your pansy mascot
you people can't kill me and
think you can kill me again
I met a tree in Amsterdam and
stood barefoot beside it for twenty
minutes then left completely restored
yet another poem not written by a poet
sometimes we need one muscle to
relax so the others follow
my friend Mandy calls after a

long shift at the strip club to say
while standing in line for death I am
fanning my hot pussy with your new book
will you sign it next week my fearless faggot sister

Camisado

after breaking in
the wolf
calmed
the hens
so he could
take his time with them
twists them open until the right
amount of memory fits into the song
another high price for belonging
poetry is the opposite of escape
but makes this world endurable
how the smallest puddle
reflects the entire sky
a return to every dream
our minds talked us out of
trusting our math of the star
your hand around my shoulder
poet astronaut you know I love you
I have no sense of failure when I am with you
everything matters because everything
hurts someone somewhere as it is mattering
we became all we carried into the mast
migratory patterns given to the love again
a way to end this secrecy of suffering
cut a door in the wolf so we
can retrieve our dead for
a world that matters

Visit a Living Being to Eat What Falls from Their Body

I am the
wagon wishing
you would find me
a maple left uncut
the rock that smashes nothing
seeking a god who speaks to
memories of life before
the heart's affliction
your cum tastes like
hand sanitizer what
have you been up to
when too many die
we deceive despair with love
sex with a man at a funeral
destroying death in his car
a holy perforation for a ghost
for best wish catch apple as it falls
eat seeds and worm to seal your destiny
everyone puts what they've got into the wheel
driving across America
raw imagination faster
than spirits keep up
I cannot remember
the last day a digital
watch was the only
digital object in my life
the first heart transplant
was the last day everyone
alive had hearts we were born with
something to get used to
I was only one year old

but do not remember
anyone objecting to
someone keeping their
strength with someone else's muscle

21 Corona Transmutations

for years after
  friends died of
    AIDS they still
      danced with me in my dreams
      did survivors of the bubonic plague
      dance with their dead
      who will dance
      with whom
      in a year
      let's
      keep
    safe
  dance
  together
IN PERSON

it was over half my life ago
since I told this many friends
I hope we all survive
we did not that time
but I say it again
I hope we
all survive
I hope we
all survive

7 years on the road
I am a stray cat now
but only when I am
not writing poems
I slept in my car in Walmart
parking lots across America
not one night
goes by lately
without thinking
of the many people
entire families I met
living in cars with signs
in their windshields
WE NEED DIAPERS
WE NEED FOOD

every man in the
UFO documentary is
sexy except the one who does not believe
a stingy imagination is unsexy
possibly the unsexiest
okay
I will
sing
out
the
window
with you
if we promise
to do it the rest of our lives

my best ideas come with
an ear resting on his chest
a holding pattern of the dove
feel our shared thought
thicken the path
it is good to take
it easy on days
when we
remember
we are going
to die
we win everything
for remembering
we are poets

names of water and wind taper
until they resemble everything
eyes closed face tilted into rain
here is the voice to
never let us close accounts
some days I can only
watch movies old
enough every
actor is
dead
this is not morbid
it is the exquisite
transitory chewed upon
reach down pull out
everything we were
told not to touch
gears of the mountain
inside a sleeping bear

my first meal after his death
a decision to persist without him
please do not attempt to command
the common winds
language shows where we stand
it can reveal how we
care about who is
listening and
how or if we
are listening
we cannot even
be sick together
wishing karma meant
foes against the wall
mr president there is only one
body on the planet whose
gender you get to identify
after that it is none
of your business

I put my
face in a
small room
called a
scuba
mask
I have carried my room
through larger ones
what did I think
I would see as
everything
imploded
after he
died I tried
to hold him
vibrating in
the middle
of a poem
everyone is always
explaining how
different
being alone
and lonely
but the next
conversation
is how we
have no
choice
but to
die

M   drew
his   face
the day
he was
diagnosed
HIV positive
and kept drawing
as his face changed
they were sublime
like Munch's self
portrait with
Spanish flu
he called on
his deathbed
at his parents'
home to say his
father was in the
backyard burning
the stack of drawings
I wanted to make him stop
please don't he said
it's his last chance to
deny me how can
I deny him that

                                the governor
                           opened the parks
                          and golf courses
                       because it would
                    not look good to
                    open just the
               golf courses
               are they wearing masks at the country club?
               is someone spraying the balls with alcohol?
               are there funny little jokes exchanged
               about social distancing?
               clink-clink the world
               burns burns burns
               burns burns
               burns

Economic Casualties
Ailing Corporations
things reporters say in the USA
Money and its
Masters
dominate
the language
first evidence
of power we
continue to
allow them

Own Your Pussy in the Dark
was the name of a play I lost
with a box of stolen journals
the main character based
on my friend Adam a
street hustler who
died of AIDS
I miss my friend
I can still see the one
typescript in the box
Adam is my Virgil who
guides me to the 18th floor
to leap off the balcony
then climb back up
not a single scratch
to leap again
and leap again
there is a lot of
resurrection and a
revirginizer machine
and a scene where we tie
pinecones to our heads to
honor the swollen pineal gland
of the goddess but that is
all I remember about
Own Your Pussy
in the Dark

we're always
putting words
in the cat's mouth
reading Eileen Myles
poems with pussycat pizzazz
one day for one moment
I could hear exactly
what she thought
I have never seen a
human choke to death
I must keep staring to
not miss my chance
I was shocked I put
the chips down
she yawned
looked away

last spring
I counted 27
dead raccoons
in one day along
the highway killed
while looking for
love little hands
reaching out
over and
over
if you do not think there
is something positive
about this virus
we are all
hiding
from
think
of the
animals

it has
been
so long
you are a
squirrel
someone
used to feed
waiting on a bench

after inventing the chair
we built a home around it
memory of splinters from
another part of the tree
every time we open
the door we require
our imaginations to
withstand what we meet
generations later
traveling over
glinting edge of the
skyscraper we finally
appreciate true dearth

my grandmother Pearl said
throw your wallet away the
moment you lose your job
there were many excuses for
losing jobs where I grew up
she was the only
person in my family
in the 1980s who asked
about my dying
lovers and
friends
she said to me after
a week with 3 funerals
there was a beginning to this pain
now you know the middle but
the end too must show itself
when you survive this
love will destroy
all doubt

we had much
to leave behind
in order to follow
the river to the sea
my grandfather said
always remember you come
from people who wash after work
       migration can
       change a family
       some die before the end
       others born along the way
              I know my
              poems by
              their shapes
              and have felt
              their edges in
              my dreams the
              side of a poem
              rubbed against
              my cheek like a
              bone comb or
              a lover's toe

last year in a
grocery store
in Indiana I met
a family with a
doomsday bunker
the daughter is also a poet
poet like a rock I said
you mean unmovable?
yes until it is time to
smash the empire
her smile electrified
a future poetry
I am excited
to live
to see

no one needs to explain
we have reached a place
without comparison
there is no louder
siren than the one
outside the door
we are late
to need
no denying it
but are we ready for a
world without presidents
a day without Caligula swagger
are we ready to make a freak show of
our hearts say *yes* just say *yes*
God came down
to walk among
Herself *living*
imagined
beauty
begins
now
She
said

load your lips
with your song
argue for beauty
always argue for beauty
it is the one fight we are
forbidden to surrender
never let them believe
we know the way
out of its clutch
this above all
will help us
feel less
alone in the world
when approaching danger
we make note of when
our bravery runs out
and know the rest
of our struggle
is fueled
by Love
nothing
else it
could
be

from Resurrect Extinct Vibration

1

A (Soma)tic poetry ritual I did a few years previously to overcome my depression after my boyfriend Earth's rape and murder led me to 'Resurrect'. I was sitting on a forest floor in New Hampshire when I realized that this man I loved, who had changed his name to Earth, died from the very same wounds humans inflict on the planet: he was bound and gagged, beaten, tortured, raped, then covered in fossil fuels and set on fire. This connection brought a flood of grief. After my tears subsided, I lay flat on the fallen leaves, feeling my breath sync with the soil beneath me and with the wind, birds, insects – and as suddenly as I had burst into tears came a lavish shower of peace. It was extraordinary, instantly feeling these connections in my body. These sensations guided me to the 'Resurrect'.

At the time of finishing this book, I had been living on the road for 7 years. I drove back and forth across the United States to teach and to perform my poetry, and for the 3 years from 2018 to 2021, I did the 'Resurrect' ritual in each state I was visiting. There are many ingredients to this ritual, which I will explain. Still, the main one involves lying on the ground with speakers playing field recordings of the many birds, mammals, insects, and reptiles now extinct or significantly depleted in numbers in my lifetime. The speakers are placed by my feet first, then are slowly moved up my body, my cells incorporating the sound waves. From the first time I did this, I was shocked that instead of feeling melancholy from hearing these recently extinguished fellow-creatures, I felt joy. I was elated, as if having a conversation with dear old friends. My guilt from these unexpected reactions braided themselves with my guilt of surviving many lovers and friends who died of AIDS.

One of my goals with 'Resurrect' was to focus on an Ecopoetics beyond our degraded soil, air, and water, and to consider the concept of vibrational absence. The World Wildlife Association's biennial report revealed the most harrowing fact that more than 70 percent of our planet's wild creatures have disappeared in the past four decades. When a species becomes extinct, they take their sounds with them: breath, foot-fall, heartbeat, wing flutter, cry, and song. Their absent sounds change the collective frequency of the planet: a missing melody to melt the ice! In turn, we replace their sounds with our human din of metal, machines, bombs, drones, and cars. The altered pattern of our planet's assembled resonance is my focus. When I was born over half a century ago, my infant cells proliferated on a significantly higher wild organic vibration than the cells of children born today. 'Resurrect' momentarily returns the music of the disappeared back to the air, the body, and the land.

2

Humans have used the hand ax for over a million years. Interestingly, the design changed very little, which is quite a tribute to its form's success and use. Homophobia – a *very nice* word for Heterosexual Violence – is so ingrained, so systemic, because of its usefulness; otherwise, we would have changed it long ago. Heterosexual Violence remains a convenient tactical method to instill fear of the human body. Most people have varying degrees of homosexual desires, and outlawing such tendencies is a perfect way to encourage everyone to police themselves and one another constantly. Those who rank too queer on the spectrum are targets for anyone who wishes to violate their true desires. Like other weapons of control, Heterosexual Violence gave us empires.

Monotheism's holy scriptures have wielded this violence against queers for centuries. I have friends who are Jewish, Christian, and Muslim, all beautiful, caring, nonjudgmental people, but where I grew up in rural America, the form of Christianity practiced is brutal and terrifying. The conflation of Heterosexual Violence and the wanton destruction of the planet is in this same harsh biblical interpretation. When I was a child in the 1970s, a group of people wanted to build a recycling center in the county. Everyone in my family and the town were angry at being told that what they did with their garbage was harming the planet. At church with my grandmother, I remember the pastor angrily quoting Genesis, stating that God gave us dominion over the earth and all the creatures on it. He referred to the people who proposed the recycling center as ungodly and Communist, and the refrain of his sermon was, 'DON'T THEY KNOW JESUS IS COMING!?' His message was to live by the scripture to please God so we can be granted Heaven one day. What we do to the planet does not matter; getting to Heaven is the only meaningful goal. When I was later Outed in high school as queer, I finally fully understood just how brutal violence sanctioned by God can feel on the body and spirit. The ruling Christian patriarchy in America is a brand of sadism Europeans got rid of centuries ago.

Conversations about our planet's endangerment must occur. The practice of this work included making drawings of extinct animals on index cards and writing a short message about the creature along with an email contact. I then left these cards on buses and subways, in coffee shops, hotel lobbies, laundromats, libraries, and community centers across the nation. I replied to each inquiry as the animal, discussing the fragility of my habitat, my courtship habits, my taste in food, how I raise my children, and finally that I am dead and that my children are also dead – that in fact my species was recently wiped out. I also provided information on theories of how we became extinct, as found in reports by ornithologists, entomologists, mammalogists, marine biologists, and others who study the recent rise and fall of the many species of life on our planet.

I also filled the trunk of my car with plastic flowers and small white tags to tie near dead animal bodies along the highway. For instance: DEER / Hit And Run Victim On Route 36 / Missouri, September 2018 / Next Of Kin Unknown.

3

I became vegan and macrobiotic in 1988, when scores of friends were dying of AIDS, and I was always urging them to join me for the health benefits. I must admit that when I became vegan, it was not originally for animal rights. I now continue being vegan to be a better advocate for our fellow creatures, but as a child I hunted deer, rabbits, pheasants, and squirrels. I wanted this (Soma)tic poetry ritual based on extinct and endangered animals to include a meditation on the animals whose lives I took when I was a young hunter.

Whisper was the name of my hunting dog. After I received my first rifle at 9, she and I loved to explore the forest and meadows. When I shot a squirrel, she would retrieve it and hover eagerly, waiting for me to give her the heart as I skinned and cleaned the body in a stream, then secured it to sticks to roast over a fire. I now refer to Whisper as my Lord of the Flies companion, and she would be sad if she were alive today to find that I no longer kill and eat squirrels in the forest.

For this ritual ingredient, I drew a silhouette of Whisper with black ink. Then I made a kite out of sticks and paper, gluing Whisper's image to the front. I made secret notes on another piece of paper with words I used for her when hunting, then glued it to the back of the kite. When I sent it in the air, her rough portrait faced the sky above me, the wind pushing my secret messages into her shape on the other side. Because we lived in the country, she never knew the tug of a leash, so it felt odd having the kite pull against my wrist, but at the same time, I liked it, getting to feel the weight of the wind on her drawing. I took notes for the poem while flying my old friend above me.

In the evening, I cut her silhouette from the kite and placed it under my pillow. The dreams were beguiling: a realm of moss on tall trees, lily of the valley, and many shards of light dancing on everything. Whisper was not there as I knew her but somehow all around me. It was a place where I felt myself relax. Then I realized that I was resting in the dream where I had buried her when I was newly a teenager. I was visiting my old friend all along in luxuriant consolation! After waking, I took more notes for the poem.

There were many memories of my time with Whisper to sift through; for instance, whenever I gave her a squirrel heart while cleaning the flesh, she would run in circles around me, which widened as she ran faster and faster until she collapsed, exhausted. When I was a child, I thought she loved squirrel hearts, and that was that, but now I am not so sure. It was the only time she would run like that until exhausted. It was the heart muscle of this very anxious, speedy creature she had just eaten. Could it be she was taking on the squirrel's vibration, running with the creature's last memory of total panic and fear of being hunted?

4

For this ritual ingredient, I used two different crystals as mediums between plants. One was exclusively for indoor plants, another for wild plants.

Indoors: I placed the crystal for several hours on a potted plant's soil near the stem. Later, I held the crystal in my left hand while taking notes for the poem. Then I would whisper to the crystal to relay the plant's message to another plant, and I would place it in the next pot. When writing with the crystal in my hand, I could feel a calm conversation, concentrated on drifting through the seasons. Their vocabulary for moving through time is something I feel drawn to remember in my body while swinging my arms and walking with my reveries for this world's possibilities. I also watched Kenneth Anger's *Inauguration of the Pleasure Dome* with the indoor plants.

Outdoors: This crystal moved between wild plants, meaning only plants whose seeds were transported by birds, wind, or some other natural force. I placed the crystal near a plant for a few hours. Later, the guardedness I felt while writing with the crystal did not make sense until I realized that somebody had mowed the meadow a few feet away. How had I not discovered this straight off? There I was, the selfish human, not thinking that somebody had cut thousands of other plants to their knees, their bodies strewn everywhere, the pungent odor of chlorophyll pouring from their wounds in the hot sun.

In the past, I have used crystals to speak between trees and other plants and animals, but with this one, I found a new relationship to received languages for the poems. I can glean from them in these writing sessions; the plants tell me that their ability to change carbon dioxide into oxygen is also transforming the words I write. Maybe, a better word is *translate*, meaning the leaves are a kind of translation device. It feels like a sentence in the conversation comes back with one word changed, giving an entirely new interpretation to both the ritual and the resulting poem. The leaves tell me they are a mirror, but nothing like the kind we humans experience. While the outdoor, wild plant crystal had more life-threatening circumstances, there was beneath that a vibration similar to the indoor plant crystal's language for the movement of time, though more urgent, a pulsing pressure running through my body. I placed the crystal under my pillow so their song could enter my sleeping body of dreams, and I whispered, 'Vegetables, sisters, brothers, unfurl a bit more with me in the poem.'

5

When I lived in Philadelphia, I had a small plot in a community garden. It was a place to retrieve a bit of the magic of gardening I had enjoyed as a child growing up in the country. With an old Polaroid camera, I made a snapshot collection of my okra, beets, and string beans from their first signs of life, to their first leaves, and finally of their full abundance of vegetables.

There was a place online for members of the garden to write to other members. I disliked reading it because it became a dump for complaints and accusations: claims of someone's stealing tomatoes and other petty nonsense. When rumors began circulating that the city would sell the garden to a contractor who wanted to build a condominium, it was the beginning of the end. And it did happen. One day I arrived at the garden with my spade and plant food to find bulldozers destroying everything. That was years ago, the piles of fresh soil and worms for our garden plots long gone now.

For the 'Resurrect' ritual, I took the photographs of my garden back to Philadelphia. At the condominium, I pushed a few of the doorbells until someone buzzed me in. I found my way into the basement, which had washing machines and storage lockers. I walked to the part of the building where my former garden plot used to exist. It was exciting being underground in the basement, and I lay on the concrete floor, looking up to the ceiling. Where there are now wires, pipes, and light fixtures, I imagined my vegetables' roots dangling above me. I brought fresh string beans, which I slowly chewed while looking at the photographs of my garden. The roots used to grip soil at this very spot, hello, *hello*, where are you now?

For several years I have been eating small amounts of different mushrooms for their various health benefits: Reishi, Shitake, Lion's Mane, Turkey Tail, Chaga, and others. They have helped me with inflammation, boosted my immune system, and provided other benefits. What we know about mushrooms and their feathery thread-like mycelium root systems, called hyphae, is that they have an ancient relationship with plants. This primordial, symbiotic connection is complex and involves, among other things, assisting the water and nutrient transport for plants. The daily mushroom consumption-saturation I have undergone these past few years has awakened my cells to the ongoing conversations between these two life-forms. For the first time in my life, I can garner messages from plants – not words, but a frequency, introducing me to my very own grand and beautiful inner-cosmos.

In the basement, directly beneath where my garden used to be, I burned the photographs one at a time. I drew a spiral on the concrete floor with the ashes, took notes for my poem, then left the building and left the city.

6

I knew very little about factory farming's brutality until I became vegan, which was in the early years of AIDS. 'Resurrect' is a (Soma)tic poetry ritual for making contact with extinct animals – of Necromancy. I also wanted contact with lovers and friends who died when we were young, people who had many conversations with me about animals' lives.

There are many dead people in my past, not all of whom died of AIDS, but a large number of these beautiful souls did. I searched for a way to contact them that was universal, and I do not mean through a kind of portal in the sense of organized religion, but something secular we had all shared or visited. There was no location I was sure everyone had seen, no restaurant or park or beach. Then I thought about how a movie could be considered a place. *The Wizard of Oz* was a film I knew for sure all of these friends had visited. I call this *The Wizard of Oz* Portal.

I have also been thinking a lot about the hypogeum in ancient Greece. Hypogea were circular burial chambers, and pregnant women would visit their dead ancestors' remains to invite them to inhabit the bodies of their unborn babies. I hope that in a past life I was a pregnant woman who performed this ritual. It sounds terrifying, seeing the bones of the dead. Still, it is exciting thinking of such an experience coursing through my electrical circuitry and nervous system, my blood pumping into the heart of my unborn child and my ancestor simultaneously.

Do you remember the film's scene where the wicked witch puts Dorothy into an opium-induced trance in the poppy field? It is an essential part of the story, because after Dorothy is pulled out of the trance, she can finally see the solutions for the way out of fear and suffering. And it is when she is asleep in the poppies that I freeze the frame, then sit across the room with binoculars, studying Dorothy while quietly invoking the names of dead lovers and friends.

One night I dreamed that I walked past a church from which singing poured onto the street. When I walked inside, everyone I knew who had died of AIDS was there. They were fantastic and laughing and happy to see me, and I was so glad to see them. There has never been a dream as good as that one for me. Even my next best dream was only half as overwhelming with beauty, hugging, and talking with these friends. If I could get pregnant, I would want to be in a hypogeum with these friends and lovers and invite them to revisit the physicality of Earth through the life of my baby. Without hesitation, I would do it and write poems with my baby, a true collaboration. I very much enjoyed writing with *The Wizard of Oz* Portal.

7

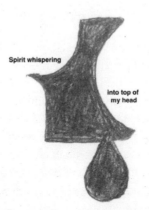

Spirit whispering

into top of my head

(shape of the poem 'Golden in the Morning Crane Our Necks')

When I began writing using (Soma)tic poetry rituals, poems became shapes. At first I tried to allow the poem to languish on the left margin, but I felt ill. Then I felt anxious while also feeling compelled to move the lines off of the left margin. The more I pushed the words into the page's interior, the better I felt.

Muses, ghosts, spirits: I have no doubt of their existence. On occasion, I have met people who say they do not believe, and I am okay with that. For those who do believe in spirits who guide us in our poems, let me share a couple of things. One morning as I was waking, a voice came to me from the dimension I was, upon waking, about to leave. The voice said, 'You have too many straight lines in your human world. We want to show you the way out of the violence of the line.' After that, I never again resisted shaping the poems, and I was eager to allow all the help they wanted to offer.

Another morning the voice said, 'The shape of a poem is the space between us. The poems are the bridge we use to one another.' Who are you? 'Many,' was the answer. Many? I began thinking of all the beautiful people I knew who died, not just grandparents, whom I also loved, but the many souls I knew who died of AIDS. Painters, singers, prostitutes, janitors, poets, the many who died were somehow pushing up to my ear, to my hair and face, singing a little song for me to translate. From 1975 to 2005, they allowed me to write most of my poems on the left margin. Since 2005 they have wanted me to explore the broader reasons I find sustenance and strength in the poem's work.

8

My first crystal has been with me for 36 years. It was a gift, a large and exquisite piece of amethyst from my dear friend Peppy, who died of AIDS a few years later. She was a transwoman many of us young queers went to for comfort and guidance, our New Age Queen. She taught me to read tarot. She also requested that I create a ritual by which to masturbate her penis one last time before what we now call *Gender Confirmation Surgery*. She not only introduced me to the amethyst, she taught me how to live with it, and how to breathe and heal with it. We had many sick lovers and friends dying around us at the time, and the things she taught me are as vital today as they were when I first worked with her as a teenager.

I dedicate this ritual ingredient of 'Resurrect' to Peppy. I took 4 solid copper water bottles and placed 9 crystals in each: 3 of amethyst, 3 of carnelian, and 3 rose quartz. Each container was then filled with water and sealed. I buried one in

Minneapolis, one in Memphis, and one in Cheyenne, forming a triangle. The fourth was buried in Omaha, situated in the center of the triangle, and I called it The Seat Of The Crystal Grid.

In Omaha, I buried the container in a secluded edge of a field just outside the city. I would get naked and sit with the crystal-filled copper container directly beneath me, and with a compass, I would align myself with Minneapolis. I then ate small amounts of dirt from the Minneapolis site and listened to an ambient recording I made at the location. Once I felt attuned, I flooded my body with the recordings of recently extinct animals while writing. Then I would turn clockwise toward Memphis, eat a little dirt from the Memphis location, and listen to the site's ambient recording. After writing, I would shift position facing Cheyenne to repeat the process of dirt and recordings and writing. In the fall of 2019, I dug up the containers, brought them to Philadelphia, and left the crystals on the doorstep to Peppy's old building. My love to you, dear friend, teacher, sister, until we meet again in the next life.

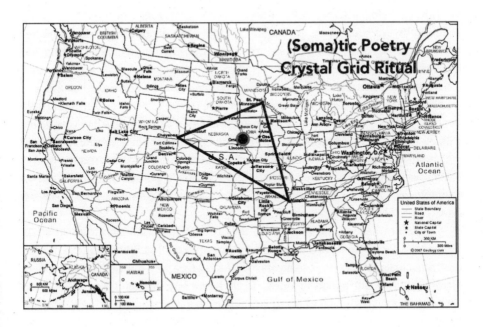

9

Walmart is a chain of retail stores with over 9,000 locations in the lower 48 states. They are massive: the average store sells hundreds of thousands of items, and the larger stores can hold more than half a million products. Sleeping in your vehicle overnight is permitted at most locations, and as a result, there is often a handful of giant, expensive travel vans parked together. There are also poor people living in cars, sometimes entire families.

When I woke in the morning, I would study the terrain surrounding the store with binoculars. If I were in Florida, I saw palm trees; if I were in Arizona, there was desert, or in Montana, mountains towered in the background. No matter where I was, once I entered the store, it became a portal into The Walmart Dimension, with the same 'greeter' at the entrance, the same music playing, same items for sale. I would listen to a recording of extinct animals and walk in a giant spiral formation, kneeling in the store's center to take notes for the poems.

I always follow these rules for sleeping in a car: (1) Always sleep in the driver's seat. (2) Always keep doors locked. (3) Always keep windows closed no matter how hot it is. (4) Always keep the key in the ignition. (5) Always park so that the car has a clean shot ahead.

There were several close calls. In West Virginia, I had a gun pulled on me, and another time someone cut my tires. In Alabama, I woke to half a dozen young men near the car; one of them bent to look in the driver's side window. He yelled, 'It's a *dude*, not a chick!' Another yelled, 'A *faggot*!' One of them approached the car with a baseball bat, and I lurched forward, turned the key, and floored the gas. In the rearview mirror I saw them run to their vehicles to pursue me. Once I got on the highway, I kept a steady speed while my adrenaline pumped. Rule 6: Always have a full tank of gas.

I pulled myself off the road when the COVID-19 pandemic struck in 2020. (Soma)tic poetry rituals are prepared for the unexpected. I brought the 'Resurrect' ritual inside with me. For several months I stayed with my old friend Elizabeth Kirwin; this was our second plague, as we had many friends die of AIDS when we were much younger and living in Philadelphia. For decades friends and lovers have given me crystals as gifts, some crystals passed forward from those who died. I arranged the crystals into a triangle, with a giant copper lightning rod coated in gold in the center, conducting the crystals' energy to its point. The golden rod was a gift from the artist Jason Dodge. I looped a thin copper wire around my neck, and the other end around the tip of the golden rod, and would meditate for 36 minutes, then write. Several nights after these intense sessions with the crystal grid, I experienced astral projection. One night, floating above the house, I wondered if we can succumb to viruses in the astral body.

Most of the poems in *Amanda Paradise* came from giant blocks of notes that I would chip away at and arrange into poems. The writing I did indoors with the crystals was different, these poems came out whole, often with no editing necessary, and they compose the long piece in the book, titled '72 Corona Transmutations', from which 21 have been chosen for this shorter selection. Thank you so much for reading.

ACKNOWLEDGEMENTS

Thank you to Wave Books for permission to include poems from *A Beautiful Marsupial Afternoon: New (Soma)tics* (Seattle: Wave Books, 2012), *Ecodeviance: (Soma)tics for the Future Wilderness* (Seattle: Wave Books, 2014), *While Standing in Line for Death* (Seattle: Wave Books, 2017) and *Amanda Paradise: Resurrect Extinct Vibration* (Seattle: Wave Books, 2021).

My thanks to everyone at UK Penguin and Wave Books for taking such fantastic care with my poems.

My thanks to the editors and publishers whose magazines and chapbooks first published some of these poems.

Magazines: *032c Magazine, Anarchist Review of Books, Artforum, Art Viewer, A Velvet Giant, The Babel Tower, Copenhagen Magazine, Lakshmi Magazine, Massachusetts Review, Poetry Magazine, Poetry Review.*

Chapbooks: *Listen to the Golden Boomerang Return* (H//O//F, 2022), *Poems for Martin, Gunnar, and Martin* (GB, 2022), *I Prefer the Forests Making Blankets from Themselves* (Bloof Books, 2023).